THE 9TH PAWN

BIG BAD MAGIC SERIES

ROSE SINCLAIR

This is a work of fiction. Names, characters, places, and incidents either are the product of the author's imagination or are used fictitiously. Any resemblance to actual persons, living or dead, events, or locales is entirely coincidental.

ISBN: 978-1-7359375-3-3
Art Over Chaos Publishing
artoverchaos.com

To my current self –
"In art we can be fucking nuts."

Part One: Shadows of The Past
Chapter One

There I was, minding my own business—well actually, following plans from a red hooded wannabe royal in the midst of a coup—when curious creatures wandered into a faraway forest.

At first, I gave the men no more attention than a passing thought, as I sat having a cup of tea in a shop's parlor. The surrounding magic trickled an awareness of everything within the forest. The whole scene in my mind took up no more focus than the drip of a faucet.

Until those droplets gathered into a flood. Sigils swam in my vision. Forgotten magic I haven't seen in a century. A burning brightness, and a whisper of words. *Dead things still live.*

"Off with this plate?" This new voice was kind, but confusingly close to what was playing in my mind's eye. Those weren't the next words uttered from so far away, but the magical tie was severed before I could sort the correct ones out.

"My what?" I blinked down, towards a piece of fancy willowware littered with biscuit crumbs. My first thought was this willow tree print didn't match the pine of that forest. And then, thankfully, my manners as a guest. "No, I got it. You've been a gracious enough host already."

I stood, carefully gathering both our plates. This dining set was old. Probably nearly as old as us. I remembered acquiring the set, just not how long ago that was.

With a gentle tip the crumbs fell off and into a small waste basket, before setting the plates on the rolling cart for a proper cleaning later.

"Don't be silly," the kind voice said, and my eyes lifted to the owner. Claudia's face was beautifully symmetrical. Soft and round, accented by wide framed glasses. The two perfect circles of glass might have looked large on her face it wasn't for the two even larger hair buns sitting below them balancing her out and adding green that never showed roots of any other color. "This is your home too."

"This is the shopkeeper's home." I paused as her lips pressed into a thin line. "You won't let me tend to it anymore."

"That's different." She smoothed the fabric of her long skirt. "You retired. How am I to learn if you don't actually step away?"

A laugh crept into my chest, and I did my very best to suppress it. She was being sincere. It wasn't her fault that necromancy was like radiation. Extra energy that soaked in based on prolonged proximity to magical things. And the shop? Well, that wondrous little store was the greatest collection of oddities one could find.

"Speaking of magical oddities," I started, and Claudia gave me a curious expression that probably meant I was replying more to my own thoughts rather then what she had said. Such things ran together. All that magical exposure makes you a bit mad. "There's a certain strangeness I need to check on."

The thing they don't teach about waking up from death is that it's like waking from a dream. One minute you are somewhere else—possibly even someone else—and the next you're not.

There's no dark silent sleep, no sense of time ticking on past you. No waiting. Just an endless stream of consciousness. It's somehow all still you, each time despite any contradictions.

I've never being able to figure out why unfinished business after your death was called *business* when they were rarely things related to profit.

I stretched out my cramping leg across the hay wagon that I've found myself in, only to realize that it wasn't the leg I had yesterday. Then glanced up to the world around me. A short way off was a long and shallow house with a sunbaked screened porch. Goats grazed within a fenced pasture that encompassed the lot of us.

Seemed I body swapped again. It might not be true for all necromancers, given I'm the only one currently, but in my 100% surveyed sample pool, it's absolute murder on your sense of direction.

When I'm awake, I can control what to possess. Last I recalled, I had been camping overnight after travelling from the shop. But the magic in that body must have ran out and moved towards this form. In a confrontation between the rock and the stream, the unconscious has a habit of going with the flow.

Usually there's some rhyme or reason for it so I mostly dwell on the lack of directions thing. Chickens are wandering the yard, pecking at the bugs as it grows dark. The smell of the crops lingers along with manure.

I know this place. It's a farm just outside the town I visited Claudia in. Outside is always easier to remember. Landscapes change less often. Waking up inside with a new body is far more confusing. Thankfully, dead things are most often kept in the open air.

I pushed myself up and out of the wagon. As I walk, I do an odd bounce in my steps to get a feel for this body. It's my preferred sex, ball-bearing, but this one frigging leg still felt funny. My steps quicken as if to hop away from the feeling as I notice a red mark on the back of my knee where there is a gash in the pants fabric. *Odd place for an injury...*

There's no blood, the mark isn't even raised. Just a little red circle that I'm sure will heal soon. I bend over for a better look and think it's a bee sting. Maybe this body is trying to give me a heads up about an allergy.

There's always a purpose to the specific body I'm in. I think it has to do something with the previous owners unfinished business or a dying wish. I actually don't know seeing as bodies that can hold souls usually only have echoes of the last owner. Nor do I make it my business, seeing as the body has been entrusted to me, and I trust it and the magic that brought us together in turn.

I stop at a creek to get a reflective look at this form. Brown hair, brown eyes. Sleeves with just the right amount of poof and tailored leather work pants. Bit boney and angular, but a cunning face. There's something missing from the whole look though...

"Ah, my hat!" I exclaim, tilting my hand up. "I'd lose my own head if it weren't attached." With a whistle, the wind picks up. Leaves that are ever green swirl around in the air

4

as a black top hat glides into my waiting palm. Upon placing it on my head, I wink at my reflection.

"Perfect. Now where were we?" I angled myself to the sun checking the direction, then aimed where originally planned the day before. "I wonder what lost thing has been found."

In the distance, along the horizon was the edge of a forest. The walk to it was dull without any conversation. Not even the voices in my head seemed to be around. Maybe the hot day made them sleepy.

I walked into the tree line, not looking back until I was certain the farm town and any hint of the rest of the world was hidden. My eyes stayed low to the ground, now searching for signs of rabbits or the holes they dug.

Once one was found, my hat was needed. I plucked it from my head and spun it toward the burrow. The black felt merged with shadows and made the rabbit hole large enough for me to jump down into.

Lost things floated up trying to find their way back as I slowly descended. Maps, books, and pictures strung and ready to be hung drifted on past.

Suddenly, *thump!* For the second time today, a heap of plants left in a pile cushioned me. I jumped up, brushing off sticks, dry leaves, and left-over hay. Then looked up at the impossible blackness above my head and waited for my equally black top hat to return.

Once back on my head for safe keeping, I ventured on down a long hall, lit by lamps hanging off mismatched panels of wallpaper. Then stopped in front of a trio of doors with a three-legged table made of solid glass sitting in the middle. On it sat nothing but a layer of dust.

But not an even layer. I leaned over to catch the light different and there was a smeared negative image in the shape of a key. Someone had been here recently. Only rabbits normally traveled these parts. I usually only came here myself to collect lost magical things to sell in the shop. The tunnels were too confusing for me to properly transverse from one hole to another casually.

Whoever was here must have used the key to go somewhere else. The doors were various sizes and could open up to endless places so without the key there was no guarantee I'd end up in the same place, even if it was the same door.

With a huff, I reached into my hat and pulled out a small vial filled with a pink liquid. I popped off the rubber stopper with my teeth, spitting it out before drinking what was inside. My vision swirled, hitting against my senses like slowed down notes. Tasted cherry tarts and buttered toast. A colorful red string appeared in the air, my fingers rose to run across it, following it to a door, and through to an engulfing brightness of the other side.

Chapter Two

A table sat under a tree amongst the others as if they simply weren't close enough to join as guests themselves. I glanced back as the red string faded from my sight, wondering if I hadn't drank enough of the potion for it to work past the door frame.

"Come closer, we shall have some fun now that you're here." A girl sat in a light blue dress with a white apron. Her hair was bright blonde as if a piece of the sky had fallen down for a spot of tea. When I didn't speak, she continued on. "It's not much of a party if no one joins."

"Is this *your* table?"

"Well…" Her eyes shifted to stare at the floral tablecloth before her shoulders lifted up to shrug. "It's certainly someone's. Look at all the seats. I'm Alice. Who might you be?"

As I pulled out a chair, I watched her with a singular focus, not even looking as I took a seat. "Do you know what day of the month it is?"

Alice considered this a little. "The fourth."

My lips parted to say no, but doubted being right. I took off my hat, placing it between several tea pots. Then reached into its mouth being careful not to look away from the curious girl the whole time.

Only glancing away as I felt a cool metal chain under my fingertips and fished out a pocket watch. Uneasy about what it was saying, I even gave it a shake before holding it to my ear. "You're wrong."

"Are you certain, sir? It must be a funny watch to tell the date and time."

"Quite."

Her eyes held steady with mine, blinking a couple times as if visually trying to translate my words. Alice's confusion only grew as I dropped the watch back in the hat and returned it to my head. "I'm the Mad Hatter."

Alice leaned back in her seat. "I was told it's ruin to call people mad."

A slight smile worked its way to my face as I decided to pour a cup of tea. "What else were you told?"

"Often before bed, I'm told that I'll never grow up. Guess sometime after that I ended up here."

I rose to my feet, cup in hand. "In Neverland?"

"Is that where this is?"

"Neverland is anywhere time stops. It might be Wonderous, it might not," I explained, and walked a careful circle around this Alice. There was no mark of magic to be found on her skin. No hidden threads connecting her to other things in this world. Not even death had marked her. Only time. "Curious and curiouser. Did you almost die, my dear?"

Her brow set tight. "I, uh, I don't think so."

"What do you remember before this?"

"I was walking down a cobble street and stopped to watch this large tower clock chime out the hour. Do you know Big Ben? Can't reason why it always catches my eye, but it does, and I always hold my breath the as the last seconds tick—"

"You're out of time." There was a breathlessness about that realization. This girl wasn't what I had expected to find when searching for once lost things. A book, maybe. Sigil covered skin of someone close to burning out on magic.

"I'm sorry, I know I ramble on and on something wild." She paused for a second seemingly catching herself. "What's your actual name? May I have it?"

"No, but you can hear it. I'm sometimes called Madison." I lower the porcelain teacup over her shoulders and place it down in front. "Drink this."

Alice's head tilts up to try to look at me, and I step off to the side so she more easily can. Unsure of what she's thinking before she decides to put the cup to her lips. "Oh! It tastes funny. Not like the stuff Mama has. Wait! Now it does, what a strange drink."

"It's tingly," she adds, and I all but ignore her as a burst of color appears like an aura. Floating in the air as if I had crushed up chalk at blew it. The colors are grainy as they float in reds, blues, yellows, before a bit of green catches on the white of her dress. Only then does time and gravity drop the floating colors onto the surfaces below.

"We must leave this place."

"Neverland?" She turns in her seat, as if to root herself into the chair. "But I only just got here."

"It's not Neverland anymore." My answer does nothing

to help her understand, but I don't care much now that time is running again. I take the chair and pull it backwards away from the table.

She reaches for the teacup again, and once it's out of reach, gives me a pout. "The other guests were much nicer than you."

I stretch an arm out, pointing into the forest to suggest she get moving. "You didn't have other guests."

"The trees were fine company," Alice grumbled as she begins walking.

Chapter Three

"Claudia!" My voice has a small echo within the bells on the door that ring as we enter. The shop is stuffed with antiques on every surface. A headless mannequin stands near the door as if carefully shopping the collection.

"Mads?" A voice calls back from behind a shelf that has a toy carriage with four horses that sits in front of a much larger model sailing ship. As Claudia steps around, her eyes go over the two unfamiliar bodies in her shop, needing no more than seconds before she recognizes me.

Most people struggle when they meet me for the 'first time' more than once. I don't think it's difficult to tell. And clearly, I'm not completely off base since Claudia always knows me despite whatever my appearance is. "Did you find the strangeness?" she asked.

"My name is Alice," she answered with a frown, looking like she has days of dust on her clothes from the travel. With bags under her eyes that soon might be able to hold as much as my hat. Likely because we did hike for two days to reach here. "I'm hungry."

"Living people have more needs, Mads," Claudia scolded as she moves to Alice as if a she's customer who has been mistreated. I wave a hand in the air, shooing any other details away from me. And wait and watch until the Claudia decides she is done fussing over Alice.

It takes too long in my opinion. A normal bath takes twenty minutes, but all the bashfulness around the body itself makes them take at least twice as long. Changing clothes only takes a few, but cleaning and drying the old dress? Ugh, I thought I'd be here all day waiting.

Finally, we sit in front of the fireplace. It's the only place in the shop with extra floor space that isn't meant to be a walking path. The hearth is filled with thin lit candles. The wax had dripped low on each making a false base that had cooled and fused all the sticks into one.

To the left is Claudia, who is very much not pleased with me right now. And to the right, Alice who is staring dead ahead at the shop's current keeper.

"You're beautiful," Alice said, then continues as Claudia and me just glance to each other. "Like... seriously the most beautiful girl I've ever, ever, seen."

Claudia smiles awkwardly at Alice, before grabbing my arm and yanking me towards her side of the large curving sofa. "Did you really have to truth tea a stranger? You could have hurt her."

"Quite humble of you to assume she's still under its effects." I glanced over my shoulder considering that possibility of accidently damaging Alice. Either via magic or excessive walking. She seems to be happily eating now so... "It's very sweet you are already worried about her, but children are not to be trusted."

Claudia tilts her head as if one of her large hair buns suddenly weighs more than the other. "She's like my age."

"Exactly. There's no telling what she'll learn to do. Can I please use that chess board already?"

"What? You didn't ask to use anything."

With a pause I replay details previously skipped over. Claudia asking Alice if she'd eaten anything. Alice saying I fed her snacks from my hat. Then citing if she had to undress in front of someone so pretty she'd die. I told her not to worry about death. Then... Claudia cooked a quote 'real meal' and now we were all here. "Oh, whoops. Can I use the chess board?"

Claudia shook her head, but a small smile was winning out. "You're mad."

"It's rude to call someone mad. Or was it ruin?" Alice said, seemingly forgetting that it was also generally considered maybe both to speak with your mouth full of food.

"My apologies," Claudia said, bowing her head a little. The gesture caused Alice to blush, and I worried she'd might choke before she finally swallowed her bite.

"I'll go get the chess board." I started to rise, aiming to walk into the back where the game pieces were kept.

But Claudia held out a hand, looking bashful herself as she started to speak, I realized it was for a completely different reason. "I... I moved it."

Once she was out of sight, obscured by curio case of glassware I leaned in my seat towards Alice. "You aren't upset at me, are you?"

This time she made sure to finish her bite before speaking. "Not really. You seem to be able to do all sorts of wonderous things. If there had been a safer and easier path I'm sure we would have done it instead trekking all that way with me."

"Exactly. You get it."

She smiled slightly, before shoving another bite in her mouth.

My eyes moved to watch the separate flames of the candles. "I hope you aren't here to kill me."

Alice made a choking sound. "Why… why would I even harm a hair?"

"Pity I'm not a hare."

"What?" A hand rose to scratch the back of her head, and quickly dropped back to her lap as Claudia returned.

She moved her teacup to clear a spot and placed the board down on the table shared between us. It was a marbled thing made from gneiss stone. The chess pieces were in a leather bag which Claudia dropped into my hand. "I don't know what you hope to divine from this."

"You, my dear, are under the assumption that Alice is our new friend." I started to explain as I took out a chess piece. Turning it around in my fingers before placing it on top of the board and followed the similar process with the next pieces. "I am not."

"But…" Alice whined, maybe remembering she hadn't convinced me before, and turned her charm towards Claudia. "You've been so nice to me."

Claudia's pressed lips had a slight squirm to them, likely wanting to side with Alice, but having seen and lived too much in her years to know I might not be wrong either. Both girls watched me carefully as I set down four bishops, four rooks, four knights, two queens, and two kings, equally divided on two sides. Then came the pawns. Eight on each front line.

I reached in the bag and pulled out an extra piece. This additional piece I held out to fire light looking to see an aura like I had Alice's before. Without any, I glanced towards Claudia. As if saying told you so, I placed the ninth pawn down in front of Alice.

"No," Claudia whispered before grabbing the bag out of my hand. Tipping it out on the table and giving it a shake. "Sometimes these sets just come with extra pieces."

Alice held her hands away from everything as if she could simply not commit. "My mom's had two extra Queens."

"Exactly," Claudia said, giving the bag an extra shake and making a wounded sound before letting go of the bag when nothing else fell out. "Damn it, Madison."

"I know." My voice was soft as my friend placed a hand over her mouth. "But you know I don't make these games."

"Wait, why can't we still all be friends?" Alice said, her voice rising above our volumes. "You said I wasn't from around here. Maybe I'm just from… another chess board. Which side is yours? I can just put 'my' piece next to it."

"Not that type of game, dear." I said, raising my neglected tea.

When I was no help, Alice's eager eyes looked to Claudia again. She picked up the pawn and hovered her hand over one side of the board as if asking if that was okay.

Claudia frowned. "We aren't on either side."

"Oh." Alice turned her palm up to look at the little piece before tightening her fingers over it. Her determination grew as she took another breath. "Well then, don't you see? This piece doesn't go to this board at all. Who knows what that means besides it's not a part of… of…"

I watched as she tried to put together a metaphor for a world she didn't understand. The words she needed found their way to my tongue. "The *current* game at play. You are part of the *next* one."

A laugh followed. This tiny sound escaped me before I even realized how funny it all was.

♟

Chapter Four

Time and I were star crossed ex-lovers. So of course, he'd leave behind a girl out of sync for me. We hadn't talked since a quarrel at a concert thrown by the Queen of Hearts. But he refuses to be beat, at anything, and the Queen of Hearts threatened my head for even attempting. But more on that, in due time.

The thing about being formally dead? Time is something that no longer touches me. If things could change, Alice would have to be the one to do it. So, what we needed was to find out what game Alice was meant to be a part of. By virtue of making her moves first, she'd have a great advantage in getting whatever she came here for.

I said my goodbyes to Claudia, then more followed, rather than leading Alice. The shop keeper's expression lingered as if disappointed that something that walked in her doors wouldn't be staying behind within the collection.

We paused under the shop's hanging sign as I tried to remember where young things went to learn. The answer lost as Alice stepped forward on the street towards rows of tables and booths filled with produce.

There were bundles of carrots, beets, and apples sitting in a wicker basket tightly pushed together. "This wasn't here when we walked in," Alice said, her hand reaching out towards the lush red of an apple.

"Don't eat that," I said, with a grimace. "It's quite old."

"Hey!" A short man behind the table objected to me ruining a possible customer.

A bowed my head towards him. "I simply meant apples are for those with decided fates."

The man mumbled a low noise, and I searched my pockets finding a coin left over and flipped it over to him.

Alice looked more curious than hungry. "If it's old, why isn't it rotten?"

"This is a Neverland Market, the most wonderous place to sell any perishable." I started walking past bright tablecloths and cloth awnings. Alice did a quick double step to catch up and fall into pace with me.

"What are the rules of this place?" Alice said, her attention quickly turning away from the market and to me.

"That depends on who the ruler of Wonderland is."

"And who is that?"

"Currently?" I spied a newspaper and ventured over to read the front-page headline before tossing it. "Seems debatable. No matter. They are all despots in the end."

Alice suddenly looked sick, and I feared Claudia had stuffed her with too much food, before remembering I was meant to be more considerate of living beings. "Don't worry, dear. Luckily, you found me first, and I haven't been bested by a single one yet."

There was a canopy of large mushrooms growing at the front of the market. Their tops stretched up above the heads of the café guests providing shade. Alice stretched herself up on tiptoe to try to peep over the edge before I gestured towards a fat caterpillar of a man. He was sitting with his arms folded, quietly smoking a long hookah in blue formal wear.

The man didn't take notice of us until we crossed his eye line. His happy expression glanced over Alice, and then me. "Who are you?"

"Still Madison, as usual."

His humph made me feel like someone who stayed out past curfew. He exhaled smoke before smiling up at the girl at my side. "Hello Alice."

Her jaw dropped. "You know who I am? I hardly know who I am in this strange place. I swore I knew when I got up this morning…"

Blue inhaled deeply before speaking, "Hello then Not-Currently-Alice."

She frowned. "That's not what I meant."

I placed a reassuring hand on her back. "Don't worry dear, things will be more normal when we leave this place. Blue, this is a *different* Alice. We need advice."

The blue in his clothes shifted a red hue, as if to prove me wrong and making his attire purplish for the moment. "No one is really different, Madison. You know that more than most."

"Maybe we should go?" Alice asked nervously. Since it had been her first real choice I did as asked without another word.

"Come back!" the Caterpillar called after us. "I've something important to say."

Our steps paused then turned back to him.

"Keep your temper," he continued, looking like a hypocrite in red now.

"Is that all?" I asked, certainly not helping his mood change back to a cool blue.

"No." When he exhaled, he watched the smoke swirl in the air. "So, you think she'll change things, do you?"

"A new era is coming, my friend."

He sat forward in his seat, squinting at me as if his eyesight had gone bad. "You never say that."

"I know. Now where should we go for *this* Alice to find her destiny?"

He placed the pipe back in his mouth, speaking around it. "Find the Wolf King, if you really think things are different this time."

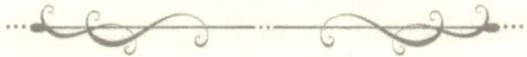

"If I found you on page 95 or so," I mumbled to myself, trying to see if the words tasted correct on the tongue. "That must mean now is page 120… 122? I might have missed something. How much time would that be? Weeks maybe?"

"What?" Alice looked over to the paper in my hands as if to read along. "How are you getting that from a map?"

"I'm not," I said, and folded the map before handing it to her since she seemed curious about it.

"You're very strange."

"Thank you. There's something I'm meant to do, but I can't seem to remember."

"We were told to find the Wolf King," Alice said slowly, looking at me if I were going mad. "Who is that?"

I snapped my fingers; certain I'd catch the answer after the sound. My mouth open to say the name, then… nothing. I leaned into Alice to tell her a secret I didn't want any soul to overhear. "I don't know."

"Have weeks really passed since I've been here?" Alice stood with one hand holding her elbow as if she'd wounded herself along our way. "I hope someone's been feeding my cat…"

"I'm sure he's fine."

"Yeah?" Her eyes lit up like a light bulb.

"Oh!" Her idea was as good as mine. I had almost completely forgotten about those men in the forest and the wannabe queen. Probably should end that deal given I was in a new body and everything. "There's someone I need to speak with before we go on. Can you wait here for me?"

Alice's expression wavered, trying to be supportive as she looked around. It was past noon, and the shadows were starting to get long. The gravel on this sunbaked road and wide-open country didn't offer much. "Okay. Don't be long?"

"My word's as good as gold." I retrieved my pocket watch from the hat and set myself a timer. With a windup, I threw my hat towards a puddled shadow, and it vanished as the darkness widened and crackled with unstable magic. With a little salute to Alice, I dived in.

Chapter Five

The shadow's underside spread out over a smoothed cool surface. I rose in a world that felt upside down until the details came into focus.

To the right, was the leader of a police force who liked to play the innocent poster child. A person worth my scorn. Sure, I had helped her get to this point, but she was beyond annoying in her habit of just assuming she had an authority over others. I had bought her schtick at a distance, but up close…

"Tell me," I prompted the red caped woman, glancing towards the men standing to my left. "Why would an anarchist care about your titles?"

"I order you to defend me!" the woman in red demanded.

I took my hat into my hands, summoning my patience since I clearly just appeared in the middle of a whole *thing* between these groups. "You've overstepped your reach."

"My reach is whatever I can take," she spat back as I

once again glanced over at the men. They looked determined as all get out. Having fought to get here both literally and metaphorically, I'm sure.

"Whatever happened to your other body?" Red asked.

I refused to even be mildly impressed with her power of recognizing me. Who else would I be? In this body, or any other. Conceding only a head tilt. "The one that made me look more like you? Didn't like it anymore."

"You used me." Red sneered, not seeming to care that she was about to just lose everything she had stolen.

I snorted at the poetry of it. The beauty in getting to start at an ending. "Let's just say," I said, taking a few steps towards the men. "I'm feeling a bit merrier than before."

Malcolm, I think that was his name. He had been in that forest, stepped forward with a literal hundred-pound wolf at his heel.

I held out an arm and blocked his path. "Death is easy. Living is hard," I said, and placed my hat back on my head. "Every monied cat and hired pig would have us eating cake all day."

The man next to these wolves, seemed to ignore me and rallied everyone to charge forward. Red sneered, pulling on illusion magic that would ruin my return to Alice, so I just stepped back and out of the way of their fray.

People were all for fighting the good fight when they thought it would bring about change. Excellent at spilling blood in the name of it, but quite shit at acknowledging the wounds it left in the fighters.

I walked around the battlefield waiting for them to stop throwing their literal lives at each other. Not that my going-ons were completely missing from this fight. My magical fingerprints where on several bodies. These must have been left over from helping Red and had shifted alliances along with me.

The dead didn't need healing, so I stopped at the wounded. Swirling my fingers to mix the magic in the air, making what already existed glow. Healing wasn't much different than necromancy in reality.

At the root, my magic made things act as if they were alive again. Pumped the heart, squeezed lungs to make a chest rise again. Both living and dead tissue reacted the same way. The only difference was if there was a consciousness around to realize it.

"Could you teach me that trick?" A voice called over.

I looked up from a body and smiled at Malcolm. "Do you know how opals form?"

"Is that the answer?" he asked without hesitation.

I laughed and started to step away. "Not quite."

"Hey, wait!" Malcolm and the same handsome fighter that had been with him before sprinted to catch up to me. "You keep showing up. Can I have a name?"

Had I? My mind asked while my tongue replied, "This bodies, or mine?"

"Ah," said the second man. "That's why Red both knew you. And didn't."

I nodded; this one was quick for someone I didn't sense a lot of magic within. Further study was needed to place him. His green hood and bow were clues. Robin Hood maybe? "The last body was called Lillie. That form is back in the ground now."

"Might be a better world if we could all change as we desired." Robin smiled softly.

"I like you," I said definitively, not minding the idea of getting to know either of these men further. "My name is Madison."

"Alright, Madison," Malcolm said, and I was curious what the sound tasted like to him. "Do you know what's next?"

"Same as always. Death and power struggles."

"Bit cynical from someone who seems to," he waved a hand at my body, but I don't believe he was flirting, "defy both."

I mirrored the gesture, only in a wider scope to include both him and Robin. They must be a thing or should be. "This is cute. I like it."

"Thank you?" Robin said, looking over to Malcolm like they'd been caught doing something more than just standing next to each other.

Alice was going to be upset with me. It was very rude of me to start a new story when I was still part of another one.

My pocket watch alarm had gone off this morning and for the whole day I couldn't summon myself a rabbit hole or a workable shadow of any sort to return.

Maybe I was meant to pay attention to the new royal court around me. But I frankly didn't. Mental capacity dedicated to sorting out the right thread I needed to follow as everything else went on autopilot. Time moved around me, more than I lived it moment to moment.

"It is customary to throw one when there's news to spread through a kingdom," said one of the princes. I think it was the charming one. He rambled on as I tried to back track to where I was now.

"Oh, oh!" I yelled. He was mentioning a ball. Parties are great for the type of magic I needed. Enough people having fun and losing themselves was perfect for whatever I wanted to do. "Might I be of help and take care of the ball for you?"

The newly elected Wolf King looked to Robin for approval. His shrug wasn't very persuasive as Malcolm worked through convincing himself.

"Just don't make this ball… dead." He had searched for a word and seemed to actually care if he offended. It made me miss Alice more.

"It will be perfectly lively." I smiled and threw an arm around Charming. He politely removed my arm; guess I hadn't given that possible friendship enough conscious effort.

The party was amazing. The biggest danger facing me was getting high off my own rocker and missing the opportunity I'd been planning for.

People are silly things. They don't know how to hold their tea. Their fear over these halls that had belonged to an oppressive queen not even a moon ago had turned into helping themselves to whatever they wanted.

"Your Highness!" I yelled as loudly as I could. Malcolm wasn't going to miss his own ball if I had something to say about it. A moment later he stepped out looking flushed.

"Finally!"

"What's going on here? Has everyone gone mad?" He asked me, as his eyes kept going elsewhere. Currently unable to believe everyone's chosen method of debauchery.

"Precisely." I leaned in to try to hold his attention, and figured he'd need a little help in order to enjoy himself. Taking the nearest cup, I offered him a drink. "Tea, my King?"

Malcolm looked standoffish, as if I had been undressing him with my eyes. He had much more lace and trappings of wealth on now. When I first saw him there had been wrinkled clothes and skin showing. That had caused my attention to skip over something important that hid in plain sight.

Being covered up now made me realize the marks on his skin had been a new addition. I couldn't spot any of the forgotten magic that burned its way into my vision before meeting Alice. Mal was absolutely right in a way; I *did* want to see him undressed.

"Just the drink," he said.

"Why, of course," I continued, as if never having asked. Seeing as I hadn't, it was easy to believe my innocence here. "Two kings are a very good hand; I'd never split the pair."

"Wouldn't three of a kind be better?"

I bopped him on the nose, and he nearly dropped the tea I had given him in surprise. "Naughty, naughty." I grinned and started to walk away. "It all really depends on what game you're playing. In blackjack, you would bust."

The real riddle was this: If Alice were to meet the Wolf King, and Mal's new depth of magic summoned her, then why wasn't he looking for her?

If Alice truly wasn't a part of his story, then had he

broken some worldly barrier without realizing it?

Chapter Six

"Honey! I'm home." I lifted a jar of disgusting bee whatever into the air as a peace offering as I entered the shop again. Then placed my hat on the headless mannequin by the door.

"I thought you were dead!" Alice said, stunned still. Her steps made quick time to make up for it, before throwing the tea from her cup onto my face.

I spat out the dreadful stuff her and her mother drank, then wiped my mouth with a hand. "You haven't taught her what necromancy is yet? How long as she been here?"

Claudia's voice didn't instantly call back an answer, so I smiled at the angry little spit ball staring me down. "Do you like honey?"

"It's thick, sticky, and gross," Alice said, and seemed to like me equally in this second.

"Well, that's good since this isn't for you. Frankly, I didn't know what to bring you, but I'm back? Did you not miss me at all?"

"Of course, I did! That's why I was so worried."

Claudia finally appeared from the back of the shop. I handled her the honey when we were close to each other. She uses it her tea to change the magic she's aiming for so often runs out. "I did tell Alice you couldn't die, least not in that way. She didn't believe me. Maybe it's because you made her walk back here on her own."

"I believe only what I see." Alice seemed to have grown some confidence since I'd been gone. I did not wonder what caused that.

"Do you believe in love?" I asked.

Alice lost her stare down, only to become incredibly careful not to look towards Claudia. "Yes, of course."

"And you don't see it right now, do you?"

Claudia made a tsk sound. "Madison, please. Don't antagonize my guests. You've been gone two weeks."

I pulled both my hands to my chest. "How do you think I feel I had to live nearly two months without my favorite girls."

Claudia rolled her eyes, before smiling down at the gift I brought her. "Thank you honey."

Alice jolted, finally glancing towards Claudia. "You two aren't…"

This poor clueless child. I leaned forward to tap my finger on the glass jar. "Honey."

"Oh, right." Alice laughed nervously as she started to turn red in embarrassment. Claudia and I had the mercy to move on.

"There's a new king." I said, and moved towards the empty couch, stretching my arms along the back.

"A king?" Claudia gave the news half a moment's

32

thought. "So, what?"

"Atta girl." She always made me smile. Most people got overly excited about a new royal, when every single one who had ever lived had been some fussy commanding ass. "This means there's a Wolf King now for Alice to actually go see."

"Can he send me home?" Alice asked, seemingly less upset at me already.

"Maybe. He's..." Finding the right word to describe someone who was filled to the brim with magic was difficult to me. It was like trying to explain what the sun looked like. "Well, warm enough towards strangers. Are you ready to go home?"

"I'm not sure." Her forehead winkled with the thought. "It might not even be possible. Or super easy to do. Knowing either way would greatly help."

"Prudent." I gestured for her to sit down. "I need your mug."

Alice leaned away, hands pulling close as hearing something crass.

"The one you've been using for tea. Not your face. While it is a beautiful one, I don't wish to drink out of it."

"Oh. I set it somewhere in the shop after…" Her words trailed off, despite both of us remembering when she last had her cup.

"Come closer."

Claudia stepped away, hopefully to grab the cup and my hat which were both near the entrance. Alice watched her go silently before sliding in on the couch. My hand lifted to rest gently under her chin. "Never apologize for expressing exactly how you feel."

"You aren't upset with me? My manners were awful."

"Were you actually angry at me?"

She struggled to look me in the eye. It was probably difficult to admit true things so close to someone, but I needed her to be brave if she stayed here. "In the moment, I was *really* mad."

"I'll tell you a secret." My hand dropped from her chin, leaning in to whisper in her ear instead. Eyes tracking Claudia as she tidied the cup and inspected my hat. "All the best people are mad. About something. Someone..."

I leaned back as my word trailed off, hand circling the air and pausing in perfect time for Claudia to place the cup in my palm and hat on my head. "The trick is not to stay any such way for too long."

Alice laughed as if we'd put on a well-timed show. "How did you do that?"

Claudia exhaled softly at the question. Something was bothering her, and another jar of honey might be needed. "He sees time differently than us. Less predicting the future and more as if having read the story before."

"And the teacup is magic?" Alice asked.

"No."

She waited for me to continue. Past the point of setting the cup on the table and hovering my hands around it as if it was a holy relic.

"You're the magic he's focusing on, Alice." Claudia seemed sad about this fact as she spoke. "Anything that can hold a memory has some. By focusing on all the times you've used the cup in the past, he can see the places you'll go next."

The two of them were being awfully distracting. I could only see *this* moment, or at best, ones that were quite similar. Ones where they sat and talked. Instead of just fighting it, I

34

sat and listened to the story the cup wanted to tell, rather than the one I wanted to hear.

The fingerprints spoke the loudest. Claudia's holding the cup out in offering. Alice's which had at first carefully never overlapped with Claudia's, but day by day they grew centimeters closer.

Then I saw Alice's lips pressed to the rim of the cup before lowering to show somewhere else. A grand ballroom with gold crown molding that was up to seven layers.

"What do you see in my future?" Alice asked, making me feel so much like a fortune teller that I thought she'd might leave a tip.

"Harts."

"What? I," Alice started to stammer, "uh, that's silly."

"*Harts*. No "e". As in the Hart family's estate. Although they'd be happy for everyone to believe the Queen of Heart's was named after her family." I shook my head clearing my vision. "Cassandra's molding is tacky. Thick, with large blank panels for where her most proud moments from her reign would go."

"Wrong details, Mads," Claudia softly chimed in.

If I had feathers, they would have been ruffled. "Wrong to you maybe. The molding is unfinished. A remarkably upsetting detail to the Harts."

"How does the involve Alice?"

I stood suddenly, startling the girl in question, but the issue wasn't with her. "Claudia, my dear. May I speak to you privately?"

Her lips pursed together, before stepping out to give me room to walk. I took the lead, heading up the stairs to the private living area. Stopping outside the bathroom near the top and being sure to speak soft enough that the sound wouldn't carry far.

But before I could speak, my head does the funny thing it does. A thread of floating color appeared connecting Claudia to something in the bathroom. It was just her, anxiously preparing the tub and using an uncharacteristically liberal numbers of bubbles.

My hand reached for Claudia's arm to center myself to the now. Not a past moment. I hadn't given much thought or meaning to the event the first time around. "Love, the point of tending this shop is so you learn to listen to stories. Understand their patterns so time has no control of you. Not make this place a museum to your own longing memories."

Claudia crossed her arms, looking down the hall. She knew I was right, so I just waited until she was ready to speak. "I know, I know. It's hard to learn like this. You got to take with you the one thing in the shop you fancied. Never had someone your age come here and stay. Live with you. Why did you have to bring her here, Mads?"

Her shoulders drooped, looking like a hollow version of the being that radiated confidence that this shop was her everything.

"We'll be leaving soon."

Claudia nodded, the movement causing a piece of hair to slip out of perfect alignment. "I need... you to promise me you'll protect her."

"With my life, dear."

"*Lives,*" Claudia insisted. "If you don't, I'm taking that hat back because it's still in the inventory records."

I leaned out of her reach. Scanning her face and seeing nothing but my friend. "Lives it is."

Chapter Seven

Alice threw up at my feet as we emerged on the other side of shadow traveling. She looked dizzy. I thought her eyes might roll up before she comedically fell over. Instead, she wiped her mouth and looked up with an apologetic smile.

"I thought you'd handle that better." Instead of figuring out why she hadn't, the sudden need to take off my soiled shoes won out. I tossed my socks on the discard pile, then checked if she was ready.

A pair of weak thumbs up was my que to keep walking. Taking the steps up to the palace with an excited pace. "This is the Wolf King's castle, my dear."

Alice paused to look up at it. She dared to look around more and ended up smiling. "I like all the plants."

As we ventured through the gardens, I found myself in need of new footwear. Thankfully, I had been around this palace enough to know the closets were open season for whatever I, or really anyone, wanted to take. Surely there'd be a nice new pair left. Or even an old pair someone swapped out.

"Okay, ready for your first solo mission?" My hands patted the top of her shoulders encouragingly as we stood outside of the large door to the royal court.

"No!" Her voice had a high-pitched whine within it. "Go over it again, please?"

"Go in there and demand that Wolf King admits what he has turned into. Tell him you've been trying to get his attention and he refuses to listen to you."

Her hands nervously gripped at the fabric of her dress. "But I haven't written him. You want me to lie?"

"I'm sure *someone* has written. Just picture that you are speaking on their behalf."

Alice looked up at me. "Claudia said people imagine fiction all the time and get angry at it as an excuse. And that we mustn't do that to each other."

"Claudia said?" Seemed she was learning important lessons after all.

I walked in front of Alice with my hands pressed together in plea. "Can you lie just this once? I need to see if the Wolf King is different than all the other rulers. If you really have changed the cycle of things by simply being here. He's nice, remember?"

"You called him warm before."

Touché. "Are those not the same thing?"

"No." Alice was looking over my shoulder towards the door, and likely weighing what she was being asked to do in there. "Claudia said the same thing."

I tilted my head. "That he's warm to strangers?"

She shook her head, expression growing softer as if remembering the moment. "That as the ninth pawn some timeless stories might change. Be different this time."

No, those stories were full of time. On that front she was wrong. But Alice seemed to be on the same page, so I held my tongue willing the shape I wanted instead. "Exactly, so you got this?"

"Yes!" Alice cleared her throat and pushed open the doors as I stepped out of frame.

"Confess what you've turned into!" She yelled as the merry men guarding the door looked beside themselves with confusion.

Her aggression soon waned as she came to a stop a respectful distance back. "Wolf King, my name is Alice. I've written to you and nothing. Now my demands are far more."

Robin stepped forward off the dais, and in front of the King and his wolf familiar. Making this the first threat, even as subtle as it was, towards Alice since she'd been here. "And what might those be?"

Alice stared back. Probably without a single idea of what to say next.

Before it came to violence, I appeared behind her, stealing the King's attention as he rose to his feet.

"And who might you be today?" Malcolm asked.

"Consider me a stone," I taunted.

The wolf at his side snarled a warning. "Why are you here?" Malcolm asked. "Does this teenager wish to rule?"

I found it funny that he barely looked at Alice, even as he spoke about her. "Don't be silly, Mal. People don't just become Queen."

Magic pooled in his palm, dripping off the fingertips. I wondered what he thought it looked like. To me, it was this oil slick prism. Something he shouldn't be able to pull up so easily.

I scooted Alice forward towards him. "She just wants to go home."

"This is a strange land you have," Alice told the King. "I'm not sure I'm meant to be here."

Mal sighed, as his rage pulled back with a clear effort to stay in control. "That's why you brought her to me? Thinking I'd empathize?"

My head peaked over her shoulder. "Don't you?"

Robin scuffed. "This is nonsense."

"You're up to something, Hatter," The King went on, not even nibbling at the bait I had been told to put in front of him. The Queen of Hearts would have already tried to cleave Alice's pretty head off her shoulders. "No one changes sides this often without their own agenda. And I'm going to figure out what that is."

My hand came to rest on my collar bone. *Rude.* To think I was anyone's side was ridiculous. All the stories played out the same. What did it matter which side had a boost from time to time? "I merely wished to see if the Big Bad King was following the same patterns as before."

"Just stop." Robin readied his bow, holding it low in final warning. "Get out of our house."

Alice glanced up at me. "We should learn not to make such personal remarks," she said, sounding only like herself now. "It's rude."

"Perhaps, dear child."

I had looked away, but the weight of the King's focus on me was heavy as he spoke. "This isn't over."

"We'll see." I took off my hat and plopped it straight down on Alice's head as a poof of magic made the ends of her hair lift up.

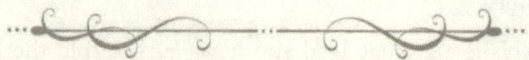

Alice threw up *near* my feet as I had the proper sense to take a step back as we emerged on the other side of shadow traveling. Well, it was more of a dry heave really as her stomach reached for anything that it could spit up this time.

"*Really* thought if I just put the hat on you that wouldn't happen."

"Madi!" She whined, and this time leaned into being crouched over, and came to a soft sit on the dirt ground.

I blinked. "You called me Madi."

"I'm sorry?"

"No, *I'm* sorry." I took a seat next to her. She'd been nothing but respectful and a good guest to Claudia, I could be gentler with her weak stomach. "We won't travel around that way anymore. Other people make do without, so can we."

"Really?"

My nod didn't change her uncertain expression, so I went on. "Whatever you want from here on out. You make the rules between us."

"So, if I said I wanted to go home, you'd figure it out? Or wanted to hang out with Claudia more. Or… I don't know." She waved in front of her to the grassy landscape we appeared in. In the distance was a sculpted hedge, a sure sign of other people.

"I'm not the biggest fan of not knowing but might be fun with you."

"Sitting," Alice declared. "Sitting is good for now."

I glanced over how she sat and mirrored her perfectly causing a giggle that I was unable to copy. "What? I'm being serious."

Alice laughed again. A short trill that got the last giggles out. "You don't need to follow me so exact. Be... *you.*" She smiled, and I understood why Claudia was so smitten with her. There were no calculations, just a queer earnestness in the curious way she went about things.

"In that case, I'll lie down." I stretched out in the grass, tilting my head back until the world was upside down.

"Do you sleep?"

"I don't *need* to."

Alice nodded as if I had been teaching her multiplication tables that were finally making sense. "Claudia said she doesn't need to sleep either but likes to."

"Sleeping is when your mind moves memories around. It's important for most people."

"But not you?"

"No," I said, sitting up on my elbows. "I sleep when I'm bored."

"I do that too sometimes." She smiled, clearly still amused with me. "I think I'm ready to venture on."

With a hop, I was up, and offered her a hand in case she was underestimating how queasy she was. "Where to?"

"Um..." Alice considered it a bit after the help up. "That

way?" She pointed towards an area full of cloud cover. Fog blurred the line of where the sky started.

"Love it, why?"

"Huh?" She glanced over.

"Most people see spooky cloud cover and think something is evil about the area. I wanted to know what you saw there."

"Oh!" Alice smiled. "I like rain."

I hummed my approval, and hoped these new shoes were good for walking.

♟

Chapter Eight

The shoes were rubbish. Never trust the rich to keep something that has more function than fashion. I carried them along with me as I walked bare foot towards the cloudy skies Alice wished to be under.

We didn't end up finding rain, but a small village outside a grove of beanstalks. There was a boy on the path walking the opposite direction towards us, pulling along a cow behind him. His head was drooped low as he muttered something to himself.

"Hey, what's the matter?" Alice asked.

The boy lifted his head, frown only deepening. "I was meant to sell this cow in town today, but no one wanted it."

The dairy cattle looked a little slim, but nothing a week of proper grazing couldn't fix by adding more fat to fill out its frame. "Why didn't it sell?"

"I told people Mama wanted to sell it because it doesn't make milk anymore." He glanced back at the cow, before sighing heavily. "Maybe I should have lied."

Alice's expression mirrored his, and I feared the boy's upset was contagious.

"What's your name?"

"Jack."

"Okay, Jack." I held the shoes out towards him. "Deed done. You've just sold the cow for these."

"Shoes?" Jack took them from me, inspecting the gold threaded loafers, unsure of their worth.

"Barely used, straight from the Queen's castle. Surely, that's better than a cow you have no use for."

Jack seemed to consider this. Glancing from the aging cow to the newness of something fancy and in his hands. "Alright, thank you."

"You're welcome." Alice smiled.

I started walking ahead leaving both the boy and cow behind.

"Wait! Aren't we taking it with us?"

I looked back to see Alice had picked up the reins. "Do you have use for a cow?"

She looked over the cow's face. "No?"

"Do you want to bring a cow with us?"

"No." She seemed a bit surer this time, despite the confusion still painting her expression.

"Then leave it be. It will probably wander towards whatever it wants."

Alice worked on taking off the cow's reins before throwing her arms out. "You're free!"

The cow's nose flared before lowering its head to sniff at the ground. Seemingly declaring the liberation a win, Alice caught up with me as we walked into town.

The scent of brewing coffee reached us before we saw a man sitting behind a greasy countertop. He was brewing some alongside loaves he had for sale, and seemed to be suffering through a conversation with a woman on the other side.

"I'm telling you something is growing in the swamp!"

"Something growing, right, sure," the man mocked as he dropped sugar cubes into his cup. "Maybe you need this more than me because you must be dreaming."

"I saw it!"

"Uh huh. Why were you even in that beanstalk filled swamp, anyways?" He leaned forward on his elbow.

The woman's face flushed. "Don't worry about it."

"I bet you saw *something* grow." He smirked over his coffee.

If the woman's face got any redder she could hide among the beets the man was selling. She stormed off, bumping into Alice, and gave a hastily apology as she retreated.

"Mercy me," Alice said, further scandalized by her choice of where to venture.

"Hey, wait come back! Don't you want your daily loaf?" The seller watched as the woman left before falling back into his seat with a sigh. "I don't suppose you two want to buy some fresh bread, do you?"

"No, thank you," Alice said, and pulled out the sides of her dress in a faux curtsey before speeding quickly past the merchant.

Once we were out of earshot, she glanced back. "I don't like him. He made that poor woman upset. Things grow in swamps all the time. I don't understand why he didn't believe her."

I paused. Looking at her carefully before my eyes lifted towards the beanstalks. These grew out of sight, from the top up. Not that the man had been right to shame her, but it *was* odd that she saw anything grow from the ground.

"Don't tell me you agree with him!"

"I won't. It's just… would you like to go see for ourselves?"

"If it's not super gross," Alice said, quick to give a shrug. "Why not?"

As we neared the area, a rabbit cut in front of us. Hardly more than a blur. Alice's steps came to a fumbling stop to avoid it. "Goodness, what was that thing?"

"It's a White Rabbit." I didn't think much of it before remembering all these things were new to her. "There's a messenger service a few shops over from Claudia's. White Rabbits use an underground tunnel system to travel Wonderland faster than anyone. Sometimes they take shortcuts through liminal spaces where time is weak or isn't."

"Is that different then how we were traveling?"

"Quite." My hand paused on my mouth trying to think how to explain. The movement changed my shadow, and the words followed. "Some mages can shadow travel. That's when you dive into one shadow and come out another. You can change a shadow all sorts of ways."

I held my hand flat out in front of me, and my shadow mirrored the motion. My hand made a fist, changing the shape again. "You can change the shape of a shadow all sorts of ways. But you have to start with a shadow which is based on the light and angle and all sorts of tiny things."

"And the rabbit holes, don't do that?" Alice said, being an excellent student. "Because they are... out of time. Like when you found me?"

"Quite." I grinned, thinking not everyone could accept the strangeness so easily. "I think we might lose some time when we get closer to the beanstalks. Is that okay?"

"Sure, I got plenty," Alice said, and skipped ahead.

What a strange child, I thought, pleased to be traveling behind her.

Chapter Nine

The woman at the general shop deserved every loaf of bread, and as many secret hookups she desired for this tip. Things *were* growing here.

We spent our time tending to a newly established garden nature started. Large brown bulbs sat on the dirt, rather than nestled safely within it. Their plant-parents too high above to provide much besides shade. The magic in the beanstalks hummed in my ears like a lullaby, but I didn't believe their magic would be enough to get them to sprout without our help.

Alice claimed she wasn't growing tired, only occasionally hungry. In those times, we ventured out to the town for food. I could tell the days were changing, but Alice didn't seem to notice. Her focus narrowed to the task at hand, the total lack of a sense of time just another plaything.

"Hey! *You!*"

"Usually?" I blinked at the young boy in front of me. Jack, the one who had the cow.

"What?" He shook his head, as if determined to not let me throw him off track. "My mama was furious with me that I sold you the cow for a pair of slippers. She sent me to bed without dinner."

"That's not very kind," Alice said, sharing the objection.

"No, it wasn't!" He pointed a finger at me. "You owe me… something!"

"No, I don't." I glanced to Alice, who looked at me with bright eyes. Ever hopeful I could make everything she came across somehow better and more interesting. I pulled forward my bag, which had a nestled bulb within it. "You can have this beansprout."

"What is that?" Jack asked, if he had never heard those words together. "Is that… the swamp is full of things that color, I don't think mama would be happy if it crowded out her petunias."

My patience was growing thin, hand letting go of the bag to search my pockets, and finding a single coin left of the two cents I had started with. "Pick one."

"That's worth next to nothing," Jack scuffed. "Plant please."

I pulled the bag off my shoulder and dumped the seedling into his arms.

"Wait," Jack said softly. "Now what do I do with it?"

"Go over there or something," I said, pointing towards the castle sitting up on a hill. "Ask for a royal audience. Trade it for a wish, or whatever."

Alice nodded. "One must learn to get what they want, with what they have."

Jack glanced over. "It's a school now."

"Education then." I shooed him away. "Leave us."

I was suspended on a rope, a quarter of the way up a beanstalk when the hairs on my arm rose. A rather funny time for this body to suddenly get a fear of heights, so it must've been something else.

Too many seeds on a single stalk would suffocate the existing plant so we'd been tending to them like an orchard in harvest season. Alice was sitting securely on a branch below, ever ready to catch the sprouts I dropped from above. She had a few buckets full already ready to be taken to the ground.

A guide rope attached to a nearby stalk rippled. The movement catching my eye. "Alice… stay here."

"What is it?" Alice asked, as I slid down. "I made sure to space the new growth apart from each other."

I took one of her full buckets to buy us some time from this delay. "Don't come down."

She chewed on her lip, then gave me a nod.

I had almost hoped to see Jack coming to complain about his newest round of buyer's remorse, but what I did see as I climbed down was wrong for this place.

"You are making a mistake," I yelled. The ground tremored along with my words. The lullaby the beanstalks were singing shifted into a protective scratching sound in my head.

In front of me was the King, walking about as if he owned the place. Which okay, technically maybe, but plants can't vote and have no mind for politics. "Don't start this tale over, Wolf."

"You worked with Red against the crown," The King said, stalking closer. "Possessed dead things. Killed people. Wasted my time. Now you take seeds from the only known place of natural magic."

"That was war."

"And what's this?" Mal stretched his arms out to everything growing around us. Not a single new bloom in this patch of land. The thick stalks and fog did a good job of concealing things.

My mouth twitched, thinking of the impressionable girl above me likely watching, hearing this man's anger filled insults. Not fully, or even mostly, really about me. What did he and that cute rebel of his breakup? Even less my fault.

This new royal was quickly becoming like every other. Loud, aggressive, shouting at their subjects and expecting everyone to take it.

"You played with people's lives! Their bodies, their... everything treated like your toys. Nothing new has sprouted here in centuries. For the last time, tell me what you are doing."

I let go of the pail in my hand, sizing him up. Taking him down would be easy. My eyes dropped to the familiar at his side. I'd seen those before, but they were rarer than people. "You mean to stop me?"

"Yes."

"There's still so much you don't know about magic. To you it's this infinite beautiful thing full of creation." I walked closer. "To me, it's death. Decay. Timelessness. And time? Ho-ho, now that's an even more difficult beast."

I was in the King's face within steps. "When I have tea, it's all laid out in rippling threads through time. Would you like your future?"

"I make my destiny."

"You sure do." So much power, and so much ignorance. But it wasn't his fault that the royals who came before hid that knowledge away. Left him to blindly stumble into a taste of it. "I can show you how the story goes if you continue throwing yourself into things for everyone but yourself."

I grabbed the back of his head, held onto a tuff hair as he tried to jerk away. My other hand lifted to his ear, playing the threads of fate like a musical instrument.

"The other Hart's resent your rule. The break in the long chain of their lineage. It starts with Sophie. Poisoned by an apple as she plays with Snow White's own child. Done to convince you to sign away some freedoms least there be more attacks on those you care about. She lies in state for years.

"Cirrus so filled with guilt, dedicates his life to finding a cure. But nothing is found. Jonathan moves on first. Taking to the seas with nothing but piracy left in his heart.

"On the verge on giving up, Cirrus weeps over Sophie's coffin. He pushes the glass lid away. Knowing he's failed. With a kiss goodbye, her eyes finally open. Love always wins. Somewhere, at least."

Mal tensed, a coiled bit of energy like a pet who has been held too long. I think of Alice first. Then Claudia. Then love itself.

"And your Robin," I said, as if to remind him. The voices in my head had seen that timeline as well, and I pushed them into his head as my fingers pressed against his skull.

The Wolf King whined, twitching under the weightlessness of magic, like a drowning man deep in the ocean and dreaming of something more.

"Look at you now. So full of love."

"Why are you doing this?" His voice is a growl even as tears escape from his eyes. "What do you want?"

For Alice to be safe. For her presence to actually mean that things changed. People choosing love.

"For now, let's just say I want a happy ending. Prevent all that awfulness from happening in the first place. It can be my gift to you."

Anger rooted him like the saplings we'd been planting. A tiny seed encased in hope against the harsh world around it. "I don't trust you."

"You don't have to."

I let go of him. One hand ran up my forearm to my elbow, pulling out all the magic in the bones below. With a snap the magic breaks out as the tips of the fingers below turn a hollow blueish pale.

The arm nothing but pure magic now as I sink it into his chest. With a tug, I pull, and his heart beats in my hand. Free of the mistake he made coming here.

A wolf howls in the distance; the plants whisper how close Robin is. Maybe true love is possible. Given the chance. "Seems you've already given this away."

The Wolf King grasped my shoulder as if to keep from passing out. Necromancy kept the blood in his body moving with its own thumping beat.

As footsteps came closer, I move back like a carefully choreographed dance, mirrored to Robin's. I smiled at the heart in my palm. Such a beautiful thing that should never go to waste.

What's left of Mal's consciousness wants me gone, even if my magic is what's keeping him upright. "Now don't be a martyr. It will make this all the more difficult."

Malcolm's body relaxed as Robin holds him, as if a soul could just find refuge in his lovers.

"Mal, I'm not letting you go," Robin promised.

His eyes were correctly on the prize he wanted, rather than me. So, I hummed a new little song to myself as I reached into my pocket finding the remaining coin. "What has great value, yet worth next to nothing?"

Robin ignored my riddle as he spoke to the fading King. No appreciation for the necromantic arts. That's okay, they were still cute.

A heart sat in one hand, the coin in the other. The face stamped on it my only real audience. Some somebody I didn't really know with a crown.

Magic pooled up from my hand, into the coin, and growing liquid hot. I pushed the pain back, focused on what I wanted the currency to look like.

Once cooled, the metal turned back into a solid disc. Only the crown remained from the original image. The face on it now the profile of a skull. I looped the metal on a piece of leather string. Robin nervously watched as I stepped close again but allowed me to place the necklace over Malcolm's head.

Mal instantly seemed to have more life in him and reached for it.

"Careful with that," I warned. "That necklace now holds your mortality."

Robin pulled one of the now *former* King's arms over his shoulder. "You couldn't have left it inside him?"

I shrugged. "I made your love virtually immortal now. A thank you would be nice."

Malcolm read the extra little message I left for him first, then Robin, as he continued to scold me. "You think that's funny?"

"Yes." Only fair for me to have some fun after they interrupted my gardening time with Alice. "What can I say? I'm a romantic through and through. Wanted the ending where you two got to stay together forever. The only way that was possible was for you to die and create a new power vacuum. Oh, things in Wonderland are about to get truly mad."

"Us staying together?" Robin repeated, chastising forgotten.

Mal still looked a bit lost. "How long was I dead for?"

What a silly question. To me, not that long. To Alice, as she sat waiting probably longer. To them? Who knew. "A bit."

I sighed to myself. Better make sure this story was over so I could get back to her. "Your little Big Bad here," I said to Robin. "Was about to throw himself at a losing battle. Again. I had to make sure he learned to fight for the life he actually wanted."

"By killing me?" The now immortal objected, clearly not understanding my gifts.

"Some cycles must be broken."

"Thank you," Robin said, showing some appreciation. He was the real owner of that heart after all.

"Anyway," I said voice lifting, bouncing on my toes along with it. "The kingdom will be in shambles. Your little new magical college won't know what to do with itself. Oh, but what they could learn. Pure anarchy. Someone really should do something about all of that."

They largely ignored me. No last adventure, no last chapter with yours truly. I was as truly as free as that cow.

Part Two: Second Hands and Other Presents
Chapter Ten

A phalanx of my middle finger was broken. As well as my left radius bone, but I had known I've damaged that. I hadn't noticed the finger until now.

Alice dropped down from the beanstalk. She wasn't exactly following what I had instructed her to do, but the pair of Kings were gone, and correctly assumed my intent. "What just happened?"

"I broke bones."

"What?" She rushed over, and I realized that hadn't been what she meant. "Are you okay?"

"Yes, they will heal."

Alice took a step back from babying my hand, looking for a moment like she'd swat me. Then her expression shifted to something else I hadn't seen on her face before.

"You're..." She struggled and dared to finish her sentence. "Kind-of scary. Did you really kill the Wolf King?"

"You aren't going to hold a technicality against me, are you? Alice, come on. He's fine."

Her brow pulled tight. "Are those things he said about you true?"

"Which things?"

"That... that you possess things."

"Oh, yes." I spun around, showcasing the body I beat up a little just now. "Ta da?"

"What? That's madness!"

I blinked. It did sound rude when she said it like that.

"Alice, darling. What did you think necromancy was?" Come on, she had to forgive me, right? I wasn't the one with the familiar who would literally bite people.

"I dunno," she said, voice barely above a whine. "That you refused to let things die."

"See, clearly the good guy," I joked, giving a cheesy grin, and tried to do a flourish with my hands. "Fuck'n ow!"

"You are *not* changing bodies just because you didn't take care of this one, mister!" She pointed an accusatory finger at me. "Where I come from, we take care of the one, our whole lives."

I couldn't help but pout. It was only a few bones. There were more of those than people. They'd stitch themselves back together if I just held still long enough. "What happened to 'Madi'?"

Alice leaned in, pursing her mouth as she looked me over carefully. "You aren't very scary right now."

"Why would I be scary?"

A smile won the war for placement on Alice's face. "I suppose one shouldn't be upset over things they don't understand. At least not without listening fully first."

"You are as kind, as you are fair."

"No, no." She backed off a step. "If you are going to tell me that I should replace the king. Nuh uh. I don't want to hear it. I was having fun just wasting time gardening. People with crowns here don't seem to have a simple time."

"No, they don't. Which is why I'd never suggest such a foolish thing." I ventured over to pick up the bucket that I had dropped at the start of this whole thing. Sharp pain shot up my arm. *I know, body. I was there. Stop reminding me.*

"I'd like to be done here," Alice declared, as she fussed with her muddy clothes.

"Oh?"

"Yes," she said, looking upset that the dress couldn't just be brushed clean. "Surely there must be other new and interesting things going on in this place."

"Let's find out."

Getting lost in a rabbit hole was neither new, nor interesting, since all the tunnels looked the same. It probably would have helped if Alice had an idea of where she wanted to go.

Not that I was much help either. Wanting to follow Alice meant if she got lost, my true north just pointed towards her.

Three hours later—I was counting the seconds this time—Alice stopped near a large root that had grown out and back into the ground above us.

"Let's just camp here," she said. "Maybe when I'm less tired we can find the way."

We settled down on the floor. Alice tried to use her bag as a pillow, finding it unsuitable before testing my chest as a more comfortable spot. "Is this okay?"

Her head was faced away from me. Towards a hallway of darkness that held a soft glow from bioluminescent mushrooms dotting the ceiling like stars.

"Same rules as before," I softly reminded, "whatever you want."

She fell asleep first, and I shortly after since it was the easiest to rest a body. When I woke up as Alice shifted her weight off me, there wasn't even an echo of pain.

Alice sat there a moment before rubbing her as eyes. "You look… older."

"Do I?"

"Yeah, it's weird like you aged five years over night."

I think my lack of alarm confused her. Bodies did all sorts of things without your permission. Aging was the natural way of things. Alice looked, well, like Alice. Taking plant growth around us into account, the room looked the same as before. Just me then. "My finger's better."

"Overnight?" She took my hand in hers, feeling along the knuckle that now aligned with the others. "Does healing age you?"

"It can." It was probably passive necromancy, but all aging healed everyone with some level of effort. It wasn't something I felt particularly special in doing.

"The Wolf King called you a killer," Alice said, as I sighed heavily. "No, listen. What did you see in them that made you… you know *not?*"

"Not kill him?"

Alice nodded, as if even saying the word would make her an accessory to murder.

"They loved each other."

"Aww, that's so cute!" Her hands pulled to her chest like I had just walked in with some gift she knew she wasn't meant to touch just yet. "I want to see more of that. Show me love."

"Down here?"

"No, silly." She pointed down the tunnel. "On the other side of wherever we are going."

"Right." I stood, brushing the dirt off the back of my clothes then righted my hat. "Love."

Explaining that love was a great many things didn't feel helpful and left me without the faintest idea of where, or what, she really wanted. I walked over to the thick curling tree root that first caught my eye.

The texture felt rough, sturdier than the packed dirt around it. Only this piece could be seen of a surely expansive root system that had dug through the dirt in search of what it needed to grow a vibrant version of itself above the ground. A bit like a love story actually.

Alice clearly meant the sensual romantic kind, that caused people hold each other in moments where anything else would've been too painful.

My hand followed along the root system tracing the path it wove through the ground and out of sight. Even past the tree, I followed the guideline as Alice took my free hand.

There was daylight on the other side. I wouldn't be able to give any sort of measurement of distance. But we had moved unnaturally far in the short walk. There wasn't a beanstalk in sight and the humidity in the air all but vanished.

We strolled arm in arm through a garden towards a large estate that a rabbit hole opened up to. There was a gray brick path drawing a line around a small pond with lilies floating on the surface.

"What's here?" Alice asked.

"Love, I suppose."

There was no guard, or any other soul outside, so we continued to explore the grounds before letting a stone entrance direct us inside.

The room opened up, framed by two pillars with craved frogs sitting on top. A throne sat empty towards the back of the room.

Alice slowly walked towards it, saying something along her way. But her words were nothing but a bow running melodically across the acoustic instrument that this room was.

From further back, I snapped my fingers to test the sound. The noise was nowhere near as vibrant. What a fun throne room.

Alice was being respectful not sit in someone else's seat, which was good since two men came in as a very belated welcome party.

I watched as they continued their existing conversation midstride. Enthralled with each other and debating something I didn't have enough context for. They didn't seem to like each other's company as they remained completely unaware that we had just come in.

"Come on, wait." The cuter one said, as the other had been taking faster steps for a quick exit. "I'm doing my best to help."

The man he spoke with was picture book example of a prince. The type they'd draw to make women swoon, and therefore too traditional to be my type. He stopped suddenly, making the cutie pull up short to avoid a collision. "You're just like the other Hearts."

"I'm a Prince like *you!*" This man's style was better suited to where we were. Wearing cool grays with accents of green sprouted up against brown skin. "What do you want me to do, Phillip?"

Prince Phillip was dressed like mud in comparison. Foreign, as in dragged in from outside. "It's not helping my cause to be here, so I'm leaving."

When he turned away, his face flushed upon spotting strangers overhearing his royal little tantrum. He shot an accusatory glare back at the Frog Prince. "You could at least not continue to look for suitors while I requested your help."

The Frog Prince turned his palms up. Poor thing hadn't the fainted idea of who we were or why we were here. His stunning green eyes unable to find any clue before giving up. There was something magical about him. It was took everything to not just stroll up and find out.

"Can I keep him?" I whispered, as I leaned into Alice.

She giggled and kept her own volume low. "I don't think it works that way."

I looked the man up and down, doing absolutely nothing to defend the Frog Prince from an accusation that I'd happily make true. My eyes followed him even as the second Prince left the room all together.

"Aren't you going to go after him?" Alice asked. Anxiety was radiating off the question. It took me half a second to realize she was talking to the remaining Prince and not me.

He did not miss a beat. "Holding a royal against their will is kidnapping."

"Right, of course." Alice laughed off her nervousness and planted a handout for him to shake. "I'm Alice."

The lack of curtsey was strange enough that it held both our attention. "Henri," the Prince said tentatively, and shook her hand.

"Which make you a Prince of Heart." Up close Henri's eyes had yellow specks in them, and I was far too willing to drown in their depth.

"Is that a problem?" His gaze now surveyed me. Seemingly curious about the hat, but not giving me any clear sign he wanted any further disrobing. *Damn this body.* I would find his type and *be* it.

"No, no." I bowed my head in a delayed form of respect. "I like you. You can be anything you want."

"Right… thanks." His eyes scanned over the lot of us again before going on. "What are you doing here? I'm sorry if you travelled a distance, but I'm not looking for suitors right now."

"Why not?" Alice asked, quickly becoming my favorite wing man.

"The Wolf King is missing." Our lack of shock to his words seemed even more baffling to him. We appeared unable to do anything besides confuse him as his eyes narrowed trying to read more than we had said. "The Royals of Heart just installed him, so everyone's upset."

"Maybe he quit," I offered. "Quitting is great."

"Upsets are the best time for love." Alice continued the

hype, and even I felt she was being a bit heavy handed about it. But then again, love could be a fun game.

"It's very sweet that you brought your..." Henri looked from the sunshine that was Alice to the sprier earthiness that that was contained in my body. "Friend. But I'm not even holding court right now."

"Name's Madison." I held my hand out for him as well. But unlike Alice's unexpected shake, my hand was turned down, completely flipping the gender expectations.

This piqued his curiosity, turning the confusion into a tilt of his head. His gaze held mine as he lifted my hand to his lips. The chaste kiss on my hand made my heart beat harder. And refused to settle as magic wobbled in his eyes narrowing the iris before he pulled back.

"Seems I already disappointed one person today," Henri said, with a heavy sigh. "Why make it three? What can I do for you?"

Think before you speak. I shallowed roughly.

Alice looked toward where Prince Phillip had made his exit. "What did he want anyway?"

"You aren't the first clueless group to stumble in here. I'm starting to get worried about the spread of news in this world." We waited, and Henri scratched his face as he went on. "His amour is under a curse. The crown passing from the Queen to an unknown, and now missing, King has broken his patience."

"Oh!" Alice stood up straighter. "He was being rude for love?"

Henri glanced away, as if a ghost was in the room. "Yes, I suppose so."

"Why couldn't you help him?" Alice pushed further.

"Just because I have more magic, doesn't mean I have

the power to solve everything," Henri started, as I tried to do the math on if Alice made him truthful, or if he was just a *different* type of a royal I hadn't seen before.

They didn't help each other unless there was a profit to it. And if they couldn't help each other, they didn't just say that. The rule was pretend you could solve anything and everything. Then hold that above someone's head for as long as possible. Until the other person either gave up or you stumbled across a fix. What type of Prince got upset when he couldn't help someone?

"I haven't gotten the faintest idea of how wake someone up from a living death," Henri finished.

"Death?" Alice asked, and shot a quick look over to me. "Maybe we could help. Madi is a necromancer."

Henri jerked his head back, doing a double take. I thought he was going to accuse Alice of making up words. Instead, there was a beautiful near understanding there. "Mal's necromancer?"

"Like you," I said, lacing my words with a double meaning. "I'm not anyone's."

He smiled. "Good to know."

"Are we in…" Alice started, pulling her hands together in front of her chest.

Don't say love, don't say love.

"Business?"

Thank fuck.

If playing the professional meant more time to convince him to indulge in his curiosity of me, I could make this work. "I can do wonders. Resurrections, curses, and more. Mad Hatter, at your service."

Chapter Eleven

We followed Henri deeper inside his manor, where a quartet of musicians lifted their instruments. They didn't even get to the first note before they were waved off. "Thank you, but that isn't necessary."

The two violins and a viola look relieved that they didn't need to play on demand to announce guests. But the man at the cello sat back as if insulted.

A small band was not the usual type of personnel you'd see in a royal's home. "Might I ask where all the Cards are?"

"You don't know?" Henri asked as if I'm meant to remember something. "Weren't you there when Mal disbanded them?"

"Before the ball?" I had a faded memory of that day apart from the mention of throwing a party.

"I missed a ball?" Alice made a tsk sound, but I seriously doubted she'd have traded time with Claudia to go to one. Unless it was *with* Claudia. "Did everyone have masks?"

"Sadly, no."

Alice paused to consider this and seemed happier that I didn't forget to invite her to the cooler party she desired.

I took the moment to refocus on Henri. "If you love music enough to keep an inhouse band. Why didn't you go to the ball? Surely a Prince of Heart wouldn't even need an invite."

Henri made an amused noise at the idea of it, stopping outside a door in the hallway he'd brought us down. "I couldn't. My family would have thrown a fit if I'd been at a ball like... that."

"Should we know who your family is?" Alice asked, ruining my chance to ask, 'like what'.

Henri blinked over to her, surprised again. "No. I'd prefer you didn't actually."

I hummed a pleased little noise at the mischief hidden in his words. "Whatever you are up to, I like the look on you."

"How do you mean?"

"I feel as if should have seen you. Meet you there," I started to explain. "But didn't. Frankly, I was distracted at time trying to get back to my charge here."

"Why did you think I'd be there?"

"I had a vision of it."

His focus narrowed to just me, so of course Alice had to remind us that there was a bigger world around us. "Is this our room?"

"Huh?" Henri's attention broke away from me, having seemingly forgotten why he had been heading in this direction. "Yes, sorry."

He opened the door and gave Alice mini tour of the lush guest room. "I'll send word to Prince Phillip. He's staying in the villa. If he wants the help, I'm sure you can travel back with him."

Alice sat on the closer bed, bouncing lightly to test it. "Surely someone who stormed off only as far as a side house wants any help offered."

"Yes, yes." I tried to wave the subject away, moving back into Henri's eyeline after he moved. "As you were saying before?"

His eyes flickered over my face trying to get a proper read. "You had a vision of me?" he asked, amused by the idea. Perfect lips quirking up at the notion of it. "How often do you see what actually happens?"

How I deeply wanted to tell him it was fate. A sign that we should have been already together. But in truth…

"Can't say I keep track. They are less predictions and more, how do I say this?" My fingers fidget looking for the word. "Possibilities. In some timeline, we meet before today, and at that party instead. That version of you must have been feeling *rebellious*."

My words themselves weren't anything suggestive, but my tone? Now that made a blush appear as a stripe of color over his cheeks.

I pressed my advantage before he slipped away. "Can you give me the full tour?"

"Was entering into my house and getting a spare room for the night not enough? I even walked you here myself."

"Maybe for some, but I'm filled with questions." I leaned against the door frame, making it easier to watch for any tells. "Like why were you the one walking us here? Why keep a quartet that doesn't follow announcement etiquette, instead of a butler?"

Henri's gaze skipped past me, avoiding the question as he looked at Alice again. "Is he always like this?"

She half shrugged, half nodded in an agreement. The contents of her traveling bag were spilled out onto the bed as she popped a piece of trail mix into her mouth.

"I could ask you questions that you don't know the answer to if that would somehow make you feel better."

Henri chuckled. It's a refined pleased sound that makes me want to tease more out of him when it all to quickly ends. "What sort of questions would those be?"

"Why is a raven like a writing-desk?"

"I believe I can guess that!" Alice interjected before pausing. Her thinking face looked similar to having something stuck between her teeth. She was a delightfully strange child.

"I give up," Henri said, and I looked back over surprised by his non-answer. "What's the answer?"

"I haven't the slight idea."

He sighed wearily. "You are wasting my time." The Prince squeezed past me stepping into the hallway.

"Henri," I started, wondering if he'd allow me to drop the title. Use the moment to walk faster, or stop and demand a formal distance. Instead, he just turned to show he's listening. "Where are the workers?"

"They're gone." There's a grimace, something weighty there as he presses on. "The Queen of Hearts had been controlling the quite numerous Cards that had been here. When the magic, and then the legal contact that held that guard together, ended I grew paranoid having them around. Felt watched. And... guilty. I couldn't tell who was a spy and who was just trying to live the best they could. Maybe the only way they knew how, so I just let everyone go."

"And the band?"

"They walked in a while back. Hungry, with nothing but

some spare clothes and the instruments on their backs. So, I invited them to stay."

My eyes narrowed at his story. Royals didn't usually take in strays, and when they did, they were molded into some purpose. Unless... "Are you poor?"

"What?" His expression seemed thrown as if I had given him a completely random answer to the riddle. "Why would you think that?"

I crossed my arms over my chest. "You seem to care about random people."

"All the Royals of Heart care."

"Right, sure. Speaking of, if you won't give me a full tour, maybe you'll show me where the other Prince of Heart is?"

"You?"

"And Alice."

She leaned over the bed at the sound of her name, giving a small wave.

"Don't worry, we will tell him you sent us."

Henri shook his head. "I don't care about the credit. If you're a cynic, why any of this?"

"Oh, I didn't make the clear?" This hallway wasn't the most romantic setting I could have asked for. Any of his gardens outside would have been better suited. But this is where we were. "I want you."

Henri cleared his throat. "Excuse me?"

"You didn't seem alarmed that a man came to be your suitor, and since people travel to request to be your betrothed you clearly must be something special."

His eyes narrowed. "Are you mocking me?"

"Never."

"Then why are you implying that I'm some kind of—"

"Fight outside!" Alice said loudly, as she got up and walked over to us. "You shouldn't ever fight inside. Especially not in a tight hallway. It makes people claustrophobic, and therefore more defensive."

My head tilted, smiling. "That's the queerest advice I've ever heard, my dear."

"Thanks?"

"You're very welcome." I took my hat off and handed it to her. She held it with a look of reverence and repulsion. "Could you place this along with your things as he and I venture to speak with the Prince Phillip?"

I looked back to the man in front of me seeking his approval.

"It will get everyone out of my land faster, so fine." The Frog Prince turned, committed to walking away this time, and missing the warning look Alice gave him.

I tapped on the top of my hat. "Thank you," I said, smiling to Alice, before trotting off after the Henri.

We walked towards a horse path. Stopping near a fountain with frogs hoping happily around. The view was vast and made of several shades of green. The short grass near us was untamed compared to the bits further away. Trees broke up the patches in groups of two or three.

In the middle distance between here, and a large hedge across the horizon, was a small building with a doomed roof.

"That's where Prince Phillip is staying," Henri started, "He been having an aversion to going home. Something about it feeling like a tomb."

A tomb? Maybe I could help his sleeping princess.

"What reward do you want?" This time there was no humor, light, or magic in his words. Just someone tired, born rich, and waiting for a work invoice.

"You know want I want."

"You're much too…" Henri's lips twitched; the next word squished under a careful thought. "Young for me."

"Ah ha!" I pointed a finger up at him. "That's not the word you wanted to say. I simply must know the word you were actually thinking."

"That *is* the word I was thinking."

"One of them." I said, leaning in. "But not the first."

His eyes held firmly on the horizon. "Would you please focus on the task at hand?"

"If I try to wake this living dead girl—"

Henri turned sharply to face me. Refusing to lose any more ground in this negotiation. "*When* you wake the Princess."

"Yes, yes, fine. When I save the princess from another castle, I want something."

"A date, I know," he started, quickly flushing as I shook my head. "What? No! You're mad if you want more."

"Quite mad. But my request was not that, you dirty birdy." He clearly didn't enjoy being teased, so I didn't further. "I want the truth."

"What truth?"

"The truth about you. Starting with what word you wanted to say before young. Because I assure you, I'm the oldest person to ever walk through your door."

He flinched back as if to see me better. "Why do I

somehow believe that?"

"Because your heart," I said, tapping my own, "tells you it's true. It's the head that's confusing you. You must kill some thoughts if you wish to be free."

"Maybe some other time."

I respectfully bowed and turned away.

"Wait, where are you going?"

This curious person was very fond of pretending to be two people. But it was no use now with barely anyone around. "To save a princess, your Majesty."

Chapter Twelve

"**I** don't want your help."

"What?" Alice ineloquently followed up.

We were standing outside the ornate doomed roof that Prince Phillip had been staying under. And since we were outside, maybe Alice figured she could get into a fight.

"Last time someone strange and magical showed up, he got the royal treatment and ran off without helping," Prince Phillip claimed. "I don't think he even gave us a second thought once he had more power."

"Never trust a royal." I was angled towards Frog Prince's castle listening, but also not fully engaging, lost in my own distraction. My last words however derailed the conversation which had not been my intent. "I meant a King or Queen, your Grace."

"Of course," Prince Phillip said tightly. He had an air of a nice man to him, but one that had been hurt and left to emotionally bleed out without the help he needed.

Actually… I turned toward him, looking from freshly

washed head to dusty leather boot. There was something of death about him. Time was not healing him; I'm not even sure time had touched his grief.

"Don't you know who this is?" Alice asked, full salesmen as she gestured up as if I were ten feet call. "*The* Mad Hatter."

My eyes lifted up to look for the missing height that seemed to be a selling point, but was only able to catch the brim of my top hat in the field of my vision.

"He can do like… anything."

"Well, not *anything.*"

Alice shot me a sour look, before beaming brightly at the Prince. "Okay, not anything. But in the short time I've been around him, there's been huge beanstalks, shadow travel, a network of rabbit holes that ties all pieces of Wonderland together. What do you have to lose?"

"Everything," Prince Phillip said, deadly serious.

Alice nodded as if understanding fully. "And you have everything to gain."

Double, or truly nothing.

Prince Phillip crossed his arms behind his back, considering our offer. "Very well, follow me please."

He stepped into the small villa he'd been staying in. I expected a nice studio suite, but instead, the room was filled with extra cots taking up the free space. The staff sitting on each bed glanced back at us curiously.

A couple wore leather chest plates, and easily could be his royal guard. But others peered up from the needle and fabric in their hands with polite silent questions. No wonder he hadn't felt the need to go home yet, he had more staff here than the Frog Prince's whole castle did.

"We'll be returning to try again," Prince Phillip told his people. The woman sewing, abandoned her project on her lap, eyes raising in a silent thanks to the sky.

Alice leaned in towards me. "Whoever this princess is she seemed very loved."

I pressed my lips together. Was this the love that Alice wanted to see? Prince Phillip and his staff seemed earnest. They had all collectively lived in a tight space without despising each other. But there was no way every royal had suddenly reformed. Beloved by your own was not an inherent marker of justice.

They were quick to pack up, and we were riding towards his kingdom by the afternoon. Phillip divvied up the horses evenly, so no one had to walk. Even royalty shared today.

Alice was charmed, but something kept me from trusting him even though he was doing everything I could think of to make that a 'nice' bell go off in my head. Maybe some half-remembered thing was getting in the way.

The trip wasn't long. From the Frog Prince's courtyard, I had originally seen the border's barrier marking the exact line where power changed hands. Rose briar encircled all Prince Phillip's land. The thorny life stretched out past my eye line no matter how long we rode.

We made a bee line towards Prince Phillip's castle not even slowing down to give more than a wave to the patrols. The roses seemed to be the only thing growing. When it came to being a princely neighbor, he hid the otherwise barren nothingness behind the thick wall of protection.

Ah, Prince Phillip played respectability politics.

That's why he was on edge and accused Prince Henri of being inappropriate by us existing nearby. Also, likely why he originally refused our offer to help, until Alice nicely reminded he was desperate.

And a worried figure of the state was always quick to judgement, and violence.

Chapter Thirteen

Necromancy understandably gets misattributed as controlling death itself. But it's more akin to putting life within something that is currently dead, or near enough to it.

This distinction had me scratching my head as I stared down at a sleeping priciness that was quite notably still alive. The bed she was on was gold trimmed and ornate as a throne. Not a single strand of hair was out of place, and within her clasped hands was a rose.

The flower felt apart from it all. It aged, while she remained untouched. While the princess remained locked away in the moment shortly after befalling a curse. Making the rose bloom again would have been easy. But the magic the prince used to keep his would-be bride alive was some other type of magic. It felt sticky and laid on top of the original curse. "Do you have musicians here?"

Prince Phillip had been intently staring at me ever since he brought us into this wing of his castle. As if my simplest move would become a clue to solving his problem. But at my question he looked as if forgetting words existed. "You what?"

"No, no," I started again. "Do *you* have musicians in the castle? They could come here and dispel that magic that you used."

His eyes narrowed. "Why in all the lands would I do that?"

The only thing worse than a desperate royal is one who didn't understand what they did to the world around them. I inhaled deeply. "You connected your princess to your borders. As the flowers live, so does she."

"You could tell that jus—"

I cut him off by holding up my hand. "I can't tell where the magic goes past here." My fingers tilted down towards the flower. "If your magic was the red of this rose, together with the curse it's all purple. How did this all start?"

"With lullaby tea."

Tea betrayed someone? How awful. Of course, lullaby tea was the dangerous sort. Innocent enough to be used to help people sleep, but if not diffused within water could make people comatose.

Around us came murmurs from the gallery of people watching. Their doubts were struggling to follow along. A failure of the Prince in explaining what he had been literally doing with the land's magic. Alice took a nervous step closer to me in case the followers become unruly.

"You really are mad," Prince Phillip said.

"That's in the title." I started to pace around the altar. "There's only one option. Stop keeping her alive and maybe I can bring her back."

Gasps from the crowd surely covered some of my words, so I watched the Prince's expression to try to gauge how much he heard and understood.

"No…" The first word had been so quiet it was easy to doubt he had said it at all until his lips repeated the exact movement. "No."

"Madi," Alice said softly, "there must be something we can do." She was frowning and looked very protective over a stranger she had never spoken too.

"These stories always work themselves out if given enough time," I rambled, as everyone hung on my words.

The Prince tensed as if insulted, but he couldn't act out in mixed company. "Nothing like this has happened before."

"To you," I corrected. "Nothing like this has happened before *to you*. Tales of sleeping beauties have been told over and over. In one version she's raped and her newly born children—"

"Heavens!" Alice interrupted before she could hear the end. "That's rather grim."

"Why yes, actually." I swayed towards her. "Let's see how did other versions end? Kissing! You have tried kissing her, right?"

Phillip folded his hands across his chest. If only I had a rose to stuff in-between, he could match his betrothed.

"Right… of course you did." The magic was too tangled to see clearly. The Prince's fuse was burning, with who knew how long was left. And while I knew how many stories ended, I didn't know how *this* one did. "Do you have tea?"

"Breaks help everyone," Alice said, and stepped protectively in front of me. "Teatime is the perfect place to think of a new plan."

Prince Phillip waved past us, towards the crowd. They funneled out, although I'm not sure if it was for drinks or them to be out of his sight and leave us alone.

Visitors upon reaching Prince Phillip's castle normally were welcomed with balls, gifts, or at least a grand announcement to the others within the walls. Phillip begrudgingly had us sit down in a parlor with him and waited for the water get to hot enough to steam the tea in the first place.

I sighed. This would have been easier next to the princess, but asking if her empty wing allowed food and drink likely would have pushed him over the edge.

Once all the formatives of high tea were performed, I spilled a little extra something into my cup. It really put the weight of the situation into perceptive. The wing the Princess rested in gave off a chill I could feel from here. A bottomless pit pulling all the life out of the ground to keep someone these people could not let go of.

"Your land is dying," I said, and Prince Phillip's confirmation was an unneeded echo of already known things. It was clear the answer was not here. All this time and effort only preserved things.

Until…

Visions of the possible futures filled my thoughts. Moving past so fast I couldn't hold out any. Just knew none of them were what he wanted it.

My hand lifted, half seeing it now, half seeing it in the future. I was offering a rose out to someone. A beast… No, a man with curling antlers. I fell back into my chair as a thought suddenly dawned on me. "There's another Prince of Heart. Adam. He has music that can dispel curses."

"That's quite far," the Prince here and now said. "Could

you go for me?"

My misstep was to stare at the Prince like he was crass for being unwilling to go the distance himself. It left an empty moment for Alice to chime in.

"Sure! We'd be happy to help." Alice looked over to me, far too cheerful to realize that Prince Phillip and I grated on each other nerves. "Is it in the direction of the Frog Prince? We could stop back there first and tell him of our progress."

I *did* want to see him again. "Alright, whatever you want."

"Can we continue to use your horses?" Alice asked the Prince. Travel hadn't ever been a problem for me. So instead, I moved the undissolved sugar around in my tea into the shape of the kingdoms. We were currently near one coast, and the Beast lived along the southern waterfront.

"Madi?" Alice called.

I looked up, eyes scanning over her to backtrack. "Hmm?"

"Did you want to spend the night here then go, or go and spend the night there?"

"There, please."

Alice pushed out her chair, taking care to not make noise against the floor. She curtseyed to Prince Phillip before heading out as if the world was her oyster.

I stood to follow her as my current fate entitled me but was quite literally held back. Prince Phillip grabbed my upper arm, along the sleeve. My eyes flicked up to him in warning, but his conviction held. "Even royalty needs permission to touch things that don't belong to them."

"No wasting time, and don't let me see you again unless you have another solution besides letting her go."

"Don't see how I'm responsible for what you see." I went to pull my arm away, but he held firm as if I were a child who wasn't listening. "There's nothing of death about your princess. But you?"

I placed my hand over his, pulling up my own rage and pushing it towards the dead spot somewhere in his own heart and mind. *"Let. Go."*

The direct skin to skin contact did nothing grand as his eyes filled with water as if suddenly wanting to cry. His hand ripped away next, leaving him heaving as if fighting not to collapse in a sob.

"You make no sense to me." His words were toothless. Drained of their rage and replaced with the fear and mourning he thought he had killed off.

"That's because I'm not for you." I said, already walking out. "Come Alice, let's be leaving."

Alice glared at him from where she had paused at the doorway, before shaking her head and quickly fell into step with me.

Chapter Fourteen

Is it stealing if you asked to borrow something, but didn't get an answer? Either way, we rode back to the tell Henri about the new plan. What a pity it was that we were unable to return the horses until the we found a solution.

It was my hope that Henri greatly missed me in our day apart. Demand I spend every night in his bed to make up for all the ones we missed. But I held no real belief that my wishes would be so easily granted.

"Can I just go in?" I asked Alice.

"Sure, I'm too tired to argue with anything." Alice in equal parts fell off her horse than properly dismounting. She took the reins in her hand intent on at least walking the horse to the stables. Along her way asked the horse, "Is this patch of grass good? No? Okay maybe I'll curl up in one of those little stalls with you."

I smiled watching her go, then zipped into the throne room again with a lively spring to my step.

This time the Frog Prince was lounging across chair's arms. His eyes lifting from a book and to my entrance.

"Hello Madison."

His accent made it sound as if he wasn't saying a name at all. Rather, "Mad As Sin." Oh, how I desperately wanted to prove him correct.

"I'm here for my reward."

He grinned, as he closed the book. "I'm sure you are, but you didn't do anything yet."

"How can you be sure of that?"

"Alice isn't with you."

I loved the way he thought. But that still didn't mean I wouldn't attempt to get a blush. "The reward isn't for her. Since it's just for me and you, I figured I should come alone."

"Surely." His hips pivoted to sit more formally on the throne. "I must ask, you don't seem to be on anyone's side."

"That's not a question," I answered, walking closer until I was centered perfectly in front of him, just off the dais myself. What silly things, giving what was meant to be good and holy a few extra inches. He was beautiful and curious enough that I was even be tempted to kneel.

He licked his bottom lip, reforming the words. "Whose side are you really on, Madison?"

"Perhaps your side." I stepped up the raised steps, moving around him like a hungry animal picturing every tasty spot. "Or under you. On top. Whatever suits you best."

"That was not my request." The muscles in his throat tightened, but he otherwise kept a practiced focus looking ahead.

I stopped in his eye line. "Tell me again what you want with me?"

"I asked for help with a princess."

"Right, of course. But I don't know how to do that, so if you'd only let me serve your wishes another way…"

"The problem is, Madison," Henri started, deliberately pausing as his finger ran along the arm of the throne. Starting at the far edge and oh so gently gliding back towards him. "You look at all men like you want them."

"That's not true."

His head tilted, brow lifting up.

"Only the attractive ones."

The Prince laughed curtly. "Maybe I should consider it admirable you find so many people beautiful."

I placed my hands on each of the throne's arms and slowly leaned in. Our hands were the closest points to each other, but still a tantalizing hair's width away from touching. "What do I need to do to prove my sincerity to you?"

His yellow speckled eyes stayed darkly on mine. "Prove to me that you even believe in true love. Not romance, not sex. *Love*."

My tongue darted out, quickly catching the words I felt more. "Fine."

"Madison?"

Too distracted by the shape of my name on his lips I just hummed a reply.

"Take a step back," he said softly.

I did.

Once he was free to go again, Henri moved down the room. Voice carrying with an even perfection. "The kingdom next to mine is dying. Prince Phillip waits all day for his bride to wake, taking no risk to solve it. Wake her.

Let love win again."

I needed a seat to really think about what I was volunteering for so sat down in his throne. Legs crossing as I rested my head on top of my hands.

Henri simply turned and waited for my answer seemingly impossible to provoke. The Queen's law decreed that act of sitting here without a title was a death sentence.

"Why were you even sitting on the throne this evening?"

There was something in the air about him that provided a sense of power. It followed him, even without wearing a crown. "It is my seat."

I cocked a smile, feeling the buzz of the wordplay. Few played games with me, most just found my phrasings odd and moved on. "By chance, were you waiting in hope I'd return?"

"You forget your place, Madison."

I leaned further in as if the extra inch would tell me why those words didn't sound like an insult from his mouth. They sounded almost mischievous. A compliment for sure. "When I complete your quest, will you let me test the strange acoustics in here with you?"

He froze for a second, a clear recognition of the not so hidden suggestion. Before giving me the slightest nod that could be seen at this distance. What was it about waiting for something that made me want it all the more?

"Deal." I jumped up, holding my hands together in front of me, and pretended I'd been the one who wanted to play hero the whole time anyways. "I'll be off then."

I walked out past him and just before I left, he teased me further. "Don't take long."

The cheerful brightness of Alice standing outside wasn't what I needed next. But like the sun itself, she continued to shine of her own terms. "How'd it go?"

"A gentleman doesn't talk about such things."

"Eesh. That bad, huh?" She rolled up to the balls of her feet and fell back. "Well, don't worry. I'm sure you'll sweep him off his feet next time! Do frogs have feet? Or is it a paw situation?"

The urge to chastise her for being weird was high, but she was already off in her own head. So, I just walked towards stables to collect the horses again.

Henri's animal title was metaphorical. Just like how my heart might break if I didn't win his favor. Despite the fact that it would literally keep pumping blood as long as there was magic in the world.

Chapter Fifteen

"Are we there yet?" I complained on day two of nothing besides horseback riding. Even a direct path to the Beast's kingdom was not as quick as I would have liked. Then again, I didn't consider many places far given I rather shadow travel everywhere. Once I even used magic to get to the other side of shop instead of walking across it.

"You asked that yesterday," Alice whined back.

"Once we stop reliving the same day, I'll stop asking the same questions."

"It's not exactly the same," she said. Her hand rose to gesture around us, but since we had been traveling along the coastline there wasn't much difference in landmass. "Look it's rockier over there."

I looked to where she was mentioned. The area was mountainous, raised in a fashion that needed a lighthouse and lacked a beach. "Well, it is different at least."

We made our way further, finally reaching a bridge that broke up the repetitive landscape. It must have rained recently since flowers had sprouted on the far side between the cobble stone that led into the small town. Petals brightly showed off their color, eager for more visiting rainfall.

"I think we've forgotten to turn off somewhere," Alice said, glancing back as her horse continued to go forward. "I don't see any castles or fancy buildings."

"Must a royal need them?"

"I suppose not." She pursed her lips thinking about it a moment longer. "Simply figured it was part of the fun."

Small flower bushes lined the road. Their blue hues a lovely choice next to the pinks and whites that grew between. It was a beautiful area that made me want to pick flowers and turn them into paint.

As we reached the village square, a statue stood with benches placed around in a circle. Further ahead of us was nothing but a billowing growth of trees that reached above the current clouds in the sky.

"It doesn't look like him," a townsperson said to us, from her seat next to the statue. "At least I don't think so."

The stone figure looked more minotaur than a human. The height on statue was stretched to make him look *just* larger than life. Horns rose up from the skull and curled above the ears. There was a nick on the nose, but I believed that it was damage rather than a feature.

"It's terrifying either way," Alice said. When she gets off her horse, she still doesn't look away as if it will suddenly move.

"Excuse you, child." The stranger puffed out their chest as if this statue was her personal role model. "Our Prince is kind and just. You can take your pitchfork attitude somewhere else."

We watched the stranger pack her things and storm off. I got off my horse, and simply hoped she wasn't a stable hand.

Alice nervously looped the reins over her hands, as she watched the stranger go. "Is Prince Adam really going to look that beastly?"

"The scariest part is often uncertain expectations. So, either way I suspect your worry will lessen soon enough."

"If you say so."

Now the important questions remained. Where did one find a royal who didn't have a castle? And why had I handed him a rose in my vision? I hadn't even seen the type of flower growing here.

After a quick survey of the town, three places stood out as different than the rest. The first was this raised stage nestled against the rocky coast. Definitely magical in its own right, but clear of all people.

The second was a camp site with semi-permanent tents and a shared outdoor cooking pot. A few people were walking around there, but even with my imagination of what royalty could do, I couldn't imagine he'd be there.

The third we had passed without much thought originally. There had been a small cottage with far more land than the others, comprised of a large lawn and side garden.

Alice stepped up to the cottage's front door. Hand hovered over the door before she did a rapid knock. Her attempt at fearlessness held out for only a moment longer before she stepped behind me.

About the time I was tempted to knock again, the door opened. And a man who I actually thought looked like a colored human version of the statue stood in the doorway. "May I help you?"

"Hopefully," I started, with a smile. "We need your help for a matter of life and death involving the kingdoms."

His weight shifted, creaking the floorboards below him. "It's too late in the day for this, we can discuss it tomorrow."

"Why not now?"

"Boundaries." He said curtly, hand gripping the door a little more. "I'll meet you at the camp site tomorrow morning after sunrise."

"You're not going to invite us to stay in your home?" Alice asked.

"No." The Beast's lip curled up in disgust at the very suggestion. "It's not a duty of the Royals of Heart. The rest just think being hospitable means sleeping under the same roof. As if they were approachable enough to even have many strangers as guests."

I wondered if he was ready to move out since his words were filled with baggage.

"Do yurts have roofs?" Alice asked, sounding like a wayward riddle.

In the morning, after roughing it on a bare cot, Prince Adam came to collect us. We silently walked back up to the cottage he called his home.

Inside was a long table that took up most of the space. Kitchen in the back, and a room off to the side that must be the rest of the interior. On the table set out for us was coffee and sugar cookies that looked so appealing they might as well had 'Eat Me' written on them in frosting.

"The Hart's are looking for a way to undo all this…" Prince Adam said, starting straight into things as soon as he sat down. "Unpleasant uncertainty caused from the lack of a monarch. They are looking for a necromancer."

"Me?" I didn't have any business with that family. Hopefully never would. The Royals of Heart at least had some hints of their namesake. That family was utterly devoid of it.

The Beast nodded. It was a silent somber affair that felt like a warning. "Who else could bring back a dead queen?"

"Tell them via the grape vine that I'm busy working on my own things. I appreciate the information, but it wasn't why we came."

Alice sat down at the table and crossed her legs. "Was the Queen nice?"

"No, she was dreadful." On instinct, my hand went to rub my neck. "She cut my head off once."

Alice's face paled. "She did what?"

I ignored her concern, more worried about what *could* become a problem, than what had been. "Why didn't you think to let me know about this yesterday?"

"There are no more Cards," Prince Adam said, as he poured himself a cup of coffee. "The Hart family's control is weaker than ever. You are safe here."

"That's fine and dandy, but I don't want to be here."

The Beast blinked at me as if we really were different species. "Then why did you come this way?"

My true motives of trying to suck dick and protect my friends wasn't the type of thing you confessed to royalty. Even the type that seemed to scorn the title. The truth then, aside from my feelings.

"I tried to break the curse that befell Princess Aurora. Then thought of you. Maybe your music could help."

"I've already offered Prince Phillip my help. He simply has to come here for it."

"And you don't leave here," Alice said around a mouth full of cookies, "because boundaries."

Adam smiled slightly. "You're a quick study."

I reached for a cookie of my own, hand pausing over the tray as my eyes continued past towards the table's center piece. Sitting in a thin glass vase was a pink rose nested within its own leaves. This flower was part of my vision.

The Beast said nothing, until I pulled the rose free. "Put that back," he growled. "*Now.*"

There was nothing magical about the flower beyond its inherent beauty. "It's not found around here."

"No, it's not. Put it down."

My eyes finally flicked up to catch his stone-cold glare. "Tell me the story."

"What are you talking about?" Adam's expression looked like it fought against baring teeth. "Must I?"

"No."

The simple answer seemed to disarm him. The Beast's temper cooled to a wary cautiousness. "Fine. My first love adored them. Long story short, it didn't work out."

I waited for the rest of the story, and he grumbled before continuing. "They are imported, so I don't ever forget the feeling of being in love."

A small smile appeared on my face, and I closed my eyes and imaged dipping the rose in a refreshing pool of magic. Once finished, I reached out to hand the flower back to him. "Like you, I also still believe in love."

Adam carefully took the rose from my hand. Looking at it curiously, seeming to know it was different now. "What did you do?"

"It's a blessing. No more watching it die. This flower will not lose a single petal until you find the love you are looking for again."

He sat back in his chair, fingers curling a bit tighter around the rose since it was no longer a fragile thing.

Chapter Sixteen

I convinced Alice to shadow travel on the merit I was technically a wanted man. The degree to which the Hart's wanted me was unclear. If they were in a good mood, maybe they'd vow to give me riches for my services. But if they were in the bad mood, they could just as easily ransom Alice.

As we appeared in the shadow of a large tree overlooking the Frog Prince's pond, she grabbed onto my arm. Half bent over, seemingly unsure which way her body wanted to go. A moment later, she stood up. "I think I'm getting better at that."

"Indeed."

We ventured inside like we had the other two times, and I had expected the third to still be the charm. "We're back!"

My voice echoed around the room unheard. "I thought he'd be here," I added with a pout.

Alice thought for a moment. "Think he'd mind if we looked around for him?"

"Let's find out."

Following where he had bought us before, Alice and I once again first came across the musicians. This time, they played a happy little chime for their audience. Alice stopped to clap after their impromptu performance. "Do you know where your master is?"

"Not our master," replied one of the violinists.

"Oh, pardon me," Alice said, with a curtsey. "Um, Prince Henri. Do you know where he is?"

"We do not," added the cellist.

Alice bristled, and I gave her a gentle push to keep walking. Once out of ear shot, I couldn't help but wonder something.

"Why do you seem to curtsey to everyone but Henri? You shook his hand when you first met him. Originally, I thought you simply did both. But I haven't seen you shake the hand of anyone else."

"He seemed nice. Like you could break the rules around him without getting in trouble." She paused at the bottom of a flight of stairs. The path above us verged off in separate directions. "You know?"

I did actually. It was probably the thing that made him so interesting to me. Even though I was long past that sort of playful self-preference tests.

"Let's split up," Alice decreed. "I'll go right, and you go left."

Following her direction hadn't ever been a cruel fate, so I ventured up the grand staircase. There had been a trio of paintings on the top, each side featured more. Treating the left more like a museum than a hallway I stopped to admire the artistry of the still life scene, and some outdoor location I didn't know. Given the shadows and light that filtered through palm leaves over a seascape, I'd like to visit sometime.

As I walked down the corridor, I passed a painting of Prince Henri. The image was somber within its lavish good filigree frame. The outfit restrictive and overly formal. I'd have to ask if it was placed just off the top steps to ensure no one had to view it for long.

While searching for the Prince, I started to wonder why I felt compelled for his approval so much so that I kept returning to give updates along the way.

I liked parts of this palace, and I liked him, which made the world of difference. And what a world it was. A set of double doors opened in towards a large bedroom.

No gold trim here, instead a quietly bubbling water feature nested in the floor. Small blue-green tiles carved a path out towards a baloney where Henri was standing. Tulle hung around a canopy bed that was set against the wall, surrounded by silk that cooled the room even further.

The sheets flowed over the side of the bed, pooling on the ground like a frozen waterfall. "Your bed is wonderfully disheveled," I mused to myself, wondering what it would feel like to touch.

Unable to resist, my hand grazed under a seam. The weight of the duvet comfortably balanced over my fingers.

Henri came in from the balcony, watching me curiously as I stood next to his bed. Expression betraying no other emotion. "I was beginning to think I'd have to come find you after I heard the music."

With a flick of my wrist, the sheets were released. Pity we wouldn't be making the mess worse as an excuse to finally set everything right. "In an effort to protect love," I started, turning my second empty handed return into a win. "I've blessed Prince Adam with a magical rose."

Henri folded one hand across his stomach, the other bent to rest under his chin. "I didn't know necromancers could do blessings."

I gestured towards a love seat between where we both stood, offering it was a meeting point before stepping towards it. "You'll find me very versatile."

"Mages usually are."

I ended up in the middle, not leaving much room for anyone else. It hadn't been my original intent, but then again no one usually grouped me with other mages. Respectfully, or otherwise.

His head tilted slightly. "Something's wrong."

"It's just…" The truth made me feel as if I had dared to sit here naked. No, that would have made me feel less vulnerable. "I've run out of leads. All Prince Adam told me was that the Hart's want me to bring back the Queen of Hearts. If that's meant to aid Aurora, I'm not sure how."

"What?" Henri's face turned a bit green as if he were as nauseous as Alice before. "They want to bring her back? They didn't tell me that."

The question had started for me but didn't end up there. Henri stepped away, looking far off. Even lost before he sat in the nearest chair.

I stood not knowing what to do, then dared to fill the larger gap he made between us by stepping closer again. "I'd be flattered if you seemed worried for me. But there's something else, isn't there?"

"They didn't tell me that," he repeated, somewhat distantly before looking up at me. "I can't believe they didn't tell me."

"Do you speak with the Hart's often?"

He started to shake his head a little. But it looked more upset than providing an answer. "If you had asked me that before today, I would have said we talked too often."

Like the bed, I wanted to reach out and touch him. But unlike that moment, I was able to hold back since he seemed in no state to be comforted right now. Least not in that way. "What do you want me to do?"

His hand gently tapped his lips. "Come to the Hart's with me."

I leaned away at that suggestion. "I don't want to bring the Queen of Hearts back."

Henri stood, looking keenly focused. "Me either. That's why we will go to them ourselves. We can dissuade this plan before they get obsessed with it."

"She beheaded me once," I found myself unfortunately saying for the second time today. "Can't say I trust her family much either."

His eyes dropped to my throat for a moment. If he was thrown by the lack of scar, he gave no sign. "She outed me to my father. Can't say I trust them much either."

My hand rose to ward off the evil Henri spoke of as shock washed over me. Same sex marriage had been legal for several rulers. Had actually been common before a few powerful assholes pretended it wasn't. Nowadays, no one even gave it a thought that the Wolf King had a boyfriend.

The Queen of Hearts must have seen something queer in Henri that she knew would upset his father. At least I understood why she beheaded me. What she had done to Henri was worse. "That story doesn't make me want to offer them a damn thing."

"Would've thought less of you if it did," Henri said, as serious as I felt. "An audience with them is easy enough for me."

I took a step back from whatever this offer was. There was something about it I didn't like, but it was hard to figure out what was setting me off.

Ignoring him in favor my memories, I thought back to what I truly knew about this Frog Prince. *You're just like the other Hearts.* That's what I thought Prince Phillip had originally said to him. My ears had *added* an e.

My vision about Alice's future made more sense now. She'd been standing in front of the blank wall that was literally Cassandra Hart's unfinished business.

Once Alice knew that Henri wanted to go to his family's estate, she would too. She was a good person but would blindly trust a house made of candy.

"Fine, we'll go with you," I caved, against my better instincts. "But only because I promised to protect Alice."

"I never asked you do it for me." Henri frowned slightly, and yet *I* felt guilty for it. *Stupid feelings.*

Chapter Seventeen

"This is my new favorite way to travel," Alice said. Her skirt was swept forward in her hand as she scooted across the upholstered velvet seats.

Even the doors had similar padding as if to cushion feet that would never be so improper to touch it. Curtains hung behind the seats as well as windows to made it look as if there were more. The carriage could carry four travelers. Well, currently us three, and a large traveling case that Prince Henri brought with him.

"Can we travel this way from now on?" Alice asked, and had the good fortune of being directly across from him. "Wait, we left Prince Phillip's horses behind at the coast. Do you think he'll be upset with us?"

Henri lightly smiled as she rambled on. "I'll take it care of it. More horses can always be brought."

"Awesome." She smiled, then turned to me. "What do you think?"

"I doubt those horses even knew Phillip."

"No, you goof." Alice chuckled as she smoothed her dress out. "About the carriage."

My eyes lifted not really wanting to answer, and caught the sight of thick multi-layered crown molding around the roof. Definitely the Hart's style. "Sure is rich. Who is driving?"

"The cellist," Henri said softly, attention lingering on me. "You might enjoy yourself if you let yourself have half as much fun as Alice."

I'm not sure what was meant to be fun about traveling to the Hart estate. Meeting my partner's parents would have been stressful any day for anyone. But meeting your not-yet-boyfriend's parents when you knew you wouldn't get along was far worse. "Are you an expert in what I find fun?"

Henri's expression grew lopsided in silent amusement. "I feel like I'm getting an idea."

Wait... Was he flirting with me? For reassurance, I glanced towards Alice, who was now looking away from either of us as if willing herself into her own carriage.

The trip felt long even if it was located in the same kingdom we were already in. If distance wasn't a factor for messages being sent, I had the funny feeling that, despite a high title, Henri played subordinate to his family.

We arrived at a building that was several stories high. On the highest balcony was a guard watching the grounds. He was easy to spot, silhouetted against the candlelight behind him.

More light was burning away through the night along the exterior, collecting the brightest in front of the entrance. The guard at the door stepped forward and opened the door on Alice's side. "Evening, your Highness," he said, with a bow of his head towards Henri.

"Could you show my guest here," he replied, gesturing

across to Alice, "where the sitting room is? I'll be in after a moment."

After a nervously excited glance to me, Alice took the guard's hand and climbed down. With how slow and wowed she seemed to be over the plants blooming out front, we'd probably reach the sitting room first.

I moved to get out next but found a quicky outstretched leg across the seats blocking my path. My eyes followed the length until coming to a rest on Henri's face.

"Mind your manners in there."

"Mind *yours*." He had to realize the irony of exposing his inner thigh while asking for proper etiquette. Was this is a promise for good behavior? "Don't tease a hungry man with things I'd sink my teeth into."

"You need something…" Henri's words were softer, but clearly less of a flirt, even as his eyes lowered to scan over my outfit. I found myself doing the same as if I had sprung some sort of eye sore while traveling. My clothes looked worn, could use a wash, but weren't inappropriate for the setting.

Henri turned in his seat to open the traveling case and dug within its contents. Without another word he pulled out a white handkerchief. Then, even more curiously, he leaned forward and tucked it in my breast pocket. "There. Now it matches your hat. The key to most outfits is to look deliberate."

He was so close. Nearly contorted towards me, yet his hands only briefly touched, making me care little about his fashion advice.

"Henri?"

His eyes briefly fell to my lips, and he swallowed roughly. "Yes?"

My lungs felt constricted and remembered I hadn't yet promised to behave. He had been flirting with me between anxiety over appearances. Wrapping the Prince around my finger and walking up to the rest of the Hart's would definitely be a power move. *But…* I actually liked Henri, and maybe he liked me too. "I'll be good to you. *For you.*"

His eyes searched my face before smiling weakly. A moment later he closed his traveling case and stepped out.

We met Alice again in the sitting room, which was really a fancy name for the room after the foyer. The guard was standing at attention while Alice mirrored how stiff he was as she sat waiting.

"Go wake my father," Henri said, upon entering the room.

The guard flushed. "Excuse me, sir?"

"I said, go wake my father," he repeated.

"Right, of course, sir."

I leaned back watching the guard travel down the hall and not envying him. "That poor man. Could this not have waited?"

"A prisoner waits," the Prince said, folding his hands behind his back and lifting his chin. "Honored guests are owed a proper welcome."

Wow, okay. I had neglected to consider the possibility this had been a trap. Alice popped up in her seat, thankfully saving me from scolding myself as she spoke.

"What should I do?"

"Did your mother teach you how to be a proper young lady?"

"Of course."

"Try to quickly recall all those lessons."

It looked like Alice might abandon her mission for a moment by doing nothing. Then stood, folded her hands in front of her, and did her best not to appear bored.

I smiled to myself as the guard stepped into the doorway once more. "Introducing his Lordship, Pollux Hart."

The man's eyes glanced over us like we were furniture. "Henri, what is this all about?" Pollux's accent was thicker than his son's as if the words he used today weren't his first set.

His father had many of the good looks that Henri possessed, but pale, with grayer hair, and frown lines that suggested he gave everyone the same disproving expression.

I didn't see any resemblance to the Queen of Hearts, and thankfully when I had possibly meet him before it was in a different body. The both of them always seemed devoid of magic. Less unable to cast, and more unwilling to ever try.

"Father, may I introduce the necromancer you were looking for?" Henri's arm bent up, hand gently twisting in my direction. "Your letter must have gotten lost. I hadn't realized you were looking for one until the Beast mentioned that a Hart already found one."

Alice opened her mouth to speak, but quickly fixed the lapse in manners. Not that I blamed her since that was an effortless load of twisted truth.

"One can never trust the mail these days," Pollux said, without hitch. "You've always been astute when to comes to your aunt."

Enough with the lies. I took a step forward to garner everyone's attention with the movement. "Quite fortunate to see you," I said, with a bowing like it was a performance that even the back rows need to see. "And this young woman near to me is the harbinger of change, Alice."

On cue, she curtseyed. "Charmed to meet you. Your son

110

has been most hospitable."

"I'm sure," he said, barely holding the line of polite conversation before turning back to his son. "If only your own letter had gotten here in time. We could have out shined. Alas, join us in the morning for croquet. We'll work out all the details."

Pollux looked around the room seemingly unsure who to order about so he could get back to sleep. He settled for Henri again. "Surely, you arranged nearby rooms for our guests?"

"There was no time, Father." Henri's hands pulled forward, looking overly concerned. "Not in matters as important as returning a Hart to this world."

Pollux's face twitched into a smile. I hadn't given Henri enough credit for his skill at politics. By dawn maybe the family would give up on their plan completely, simply turned off by the amount of oversell. "I'll let you see to them then," he said dismissively, as I became the figure of his targeted focus. "Do you play croquet?"

With a flourish I took off my hat. "I'm quite good and looking forward to it."

"If you'll excuse me," Pollux finished, and the guard adverted his eyes to the ground and followed. Henri watched at the door making sure they were out of ear shot.

"Why didn't he say hello to me?" Alice's brow creased.

I returned my hat to my head. "Because 'harbinger of change' isn't a title. It's a fact that's nearly only interesting to me."

"What does it mean?" Henri said, quickly able to drop his formal act.

Alice sat back down on the small couch. "I'm not from Wonderland."

Henri blinked a few times. "I don't follow. What do you mean you're not from Wonderland? You might as well say you were born under a different sky."

"I was," Alice confidently said at first. "Well, at least a different patch. The stars don't match what I've used to."

Henri fell onto a nearby chair, hand drawing to his mouth as if his world view had been shaken loose. He looked up at me like I was a foothold to reality. "You knew this?"

"Of course." I glanced around the sitting room, noting its lack of books. On the shelves were shiny jeweled cups and things. "So, where are we staying?"

"In my wing."

"Is there more than one bed?" Alice asked. "No offense, but I'm a bit old to crawl into bed with a guardian like I had some nightmare."

"There's multiple rooms." Henri smiled for just a moment. "This house doesn't have official guest rooms. Even though my father sure loves to have people over to act as if it's a special honor to allow strangers in my rooms."

My mind flashed to the tight quarters of the carriage. "I wouldn't complain."

"Because you're so old," he teased, "or need the support from night terrors?"

Insult or not, I was too taken back by the acknowledgment. "You believe I'm timeless?"

Henri shook his head, then rubbed his face with his hands. "I believe that I don't understand the nature of either of you. And I rather have you closer to me, rather than them."

Chapter Eighteen

The Frog Prince's wing was a house upon itself, having everything without ever needing to enter another part of the manor. It even had a central lock. The Hart's didn't share much. Least not a single bathroom, bedroom, nor kitchen.

Alice prepared herself a meal then promptly fell asleep on a couch in his study. I indulged in convincing Henri to give me another tour. It was a weak excuse to keep seeing his spaces, but one that worked very well. This place lacked his soft cool style, and the bedroom...

"Henri, there's a mirror on your ceiling." The place was decorated as if someone who he never met him had designed it based on the rumor that he was a playboy.

"I'm aware," he said with a sigh. I watched him within the reflection as he worked to pretend it wasn't there. "My brother placed it there as a gift."

"You have a brother?" My eyes fell to the real version of him.

He turned to face me. "Why do you keep being confused or upset that I have family?"

"Maybe because they seem ill fit." My eyes kept being pulled up to reflection on the ceiling. "Mirrors bounce and amplify magic."

"I know how magical mirrors work." When I didn't reply he glanced to the image above. "The only reason I didn't take them down is because I'd look ungrateful and have to repair the ceiling."

What would I be doing right now if Henri was the person they made him out to be? Would we be using those mirrors or would Alice and I not have found his causes worthy?

"Would you like some tea?"

"Yes, please."

He moved to a little serving cart, placed between two seats. I silently watched as his slender fingers wrap around a silver spoon as he scooped loose leaf tea from a tin to cup. Somehow sharing this view in front of the collection was more intimate than the forced suggestions.

"You like tea," I said softly, feeling kinship over the smallest thing.

"Yes?" His paused before he poured the water in. "You're... something I just don't fully understand yet."

My eyes lifted in hope of catching his. "Would you like to?"

Henri lips parted, head doing an unclear bobble before he doubled his focus on the tea. He held his hand over a cup. Fingers floating over the air above as the water started to bubble. His hand moved away, back towards his own cup, as he heated the tea once more. What simple, useful, and personal use of something grand.

"You are magic."

"Madison," he said, laughing a little. "Stop, you're

114

making me feel like something strange."

I took the drink in my hands. The porcelain warm under my fingers as I waited for the tea to brew. "Do you not like being queer?"

"I… I like it very much." He cleared his throat, picking up his cup and gently blew on it. "I should thank you for being well-behaved. I'm certain you being a gentleman forced my father to behave as well. Despite the late hour."

"Some stories never change. The rich always like to be handled the same way."

His smile slipped away as if it was a ghost. "Of course."

"You wanted me to play this game, don't be upset because I was believable in the role." I took a sip, and the leaves held a rich excellent flavor that I couldn't quite place. "If anything, excellent roleplaying should be a perk of any worthy suitor."

Henri rolled his eyes and sat back in his seat. "I'm just so used to pretending around my family that it's odd to know that someone else does it too."

"You're definitely not the only one who pretends around here."

His cup lowered. "No?"

"Definitely not. All dysfunctional families pretend with each other. Hide things. Become unable to see the person who is actually in front of them." I gestured towards his tea collection. "Like the tins. I can't tell what each is, but you know and care because you organized them."

He took a sip, considering this. "What about yours?"

"My tea collection?"

"Your family, Madison."

"Oh, I don't have one. Least not anymore. There's a

theory in necromancy," I started to explain, unsure of how much he wanted to hear. He seemed comfortable with the topic, so I went on. "That it is tied to a spell on an ancient blood line. And those who can do it are related to some degree to *everyone* and that's why I can body swap or control the dead."

Henri leaned forward in his seat as if I had been telling him a ghost story over a roaring fire. "Do you believe that?"

"No, I am me. Not those who came before."

He smiled, eyes falling away from mine to stare down into his tea.

"I could change bodies into a type you're more interested in."

It had been a casual offer, but he bristled as if I offered to do something obscene. "No, don't do that. I'd feel bad."

"Why?"

"What—What do you mean why?" He placed his down cup as his concern grew. "Because it's not all about me, or my whims."

"You'd be the first in power to not have some preference. Red did. We weren't even into each other, but she wanted those that helped her to look a certain way."

Henri mumbled something under his breath. It flowed easily like water, maybe the lost language I had heard in the accent. "You're the second person to talk to me about her over tea. I don't want to talk about her again. This body…" He gestured at me before picking his tea back up.

I glanced down it at. My favorite part of this one was the hips that were accented in belts. All bodies were good. How beautiful they were wasn't the only worth they had. So, I can't say I've had one that I disliked.

"It's… not yours?"

116

"It's mine." I pressed my lips together, unsure how to explain the transpositional nature of being me. "There's no one else here. I can't inhabit something with a consciousness. Sometimes there's an echo. Less from them, and more half remembering something you heard about yourself."

"Like what?" Henri asked to my surprise.

It made him all the more endearing to me. "I think this body is allergic to bees."

"Bees?" He laughed. "I can't even imagine someone like you being laid low by something so small."

I finished my tea, and it clinked against the saucer as I placed it down. "It's always the small things that gets someone."

"Touché."

Chapter Nineteen

The visibility last night had been low. But I was absolutely certain this morning's sprinkling of white canopies lined with flowers were all set up before the sun had risen.

Wicker chairs were placed at tables with silverware on top. A few people had already taken their seats, but we were by no means late. A thin wood border was placed on a patch of grass contained six hoops and a rack of the croquet mallets.

"I don't think I've ever played croquet with people," Alice mumbled to herself. "I hope I remember the rules and don't cheat again."

"You cheated yourself?" I asked, and she just nodded instead of elaborating. "Henri, does your..."

It was no use. He was gone. Mentally, that is. He was physically still standing next to us. But his focus was surveying the whole area as if he would be quizzed on the seating chart.

"I should introduce you to the Duchess," Henri said,

and started walking. Alice and I managed to exchange a glance before following. "She's always in favor of anyone she meets first."

The Duchess was already sitting down at a far table, presumably for its view of the forest behind us. On her lap was a white cat, her white dress seemed to be dyed the match the exact shade.

"Madame Duchess," Henri said, then introduced us as Alice curtseyed.

Her chin raised to appraise us. "I appreciate the style of your fine hat."

I tipped it in thanks as Alice made kissy sounds at the cat. "I didn't know that cats could be so spotless," she said, eyes lifting to its owner. "May I pet her?"

"They all can be," said the Duchess growing cold, and ignoring the question. "You mustn't know much."

Henri worked on introducing another topic of conversation as the servers filed out with trays full of glass stemware. I intercepted one server and lifted their whole tray for myself. The server gave me an awkward smile before turning around for the kitchen.

"I find everything under the sun is more enjoyable with a good drink." The technical interruption was met with Henri's smile as he took two and offered the first to the Duchess. No one drank a drop before she did.

"A mage, you said?" This question is for the Prince despite being about me.

Henri nods. "Necromancy."

"A lost practice indeed." Her tone is much more approving than when she spoke with Alice. So much so that Alice reached for a drink of her own.

"Good blood?" she asked next.

119

"Can't say that was my line of questioning." Henri blushed slightly. "If you'll excuse us, we need to still speak with my father."

"Of course." She smiled with an extended hand.

He lifted it to place a single chaste kiss upon it before letting it slip from his hand. As we walk again, I grab a glass and discard the remaining tray on an empty table.

"Henri," I said, checking for is attention before continuing. "Am I meant to know the lineage of this body?"

"No, people will look for an excuse not to like you." Once he spotted his father, we course correct towards that direction.

"She didn't even give me a chance," Alice grumbled.

"That's because they don't know what use they have for you." Henri stops to look at Alice, frowning a little. "Let it stay that way."

Alice seemingly didn't know which fate was worse: Niceness because they want something, or bitterness because they don't. Either way, she lifted her drink taking a big gulp.

"Good morning, Father," Henri said, as he steps into the group of men talking. I hold myself and Alice back a step.

"Ah, Henri," Pollux said, waving him towards a nearby table. "Go hold our spot for us."

Henri nods politely, but the second he is facing the other way he rolls his eyes. Alice and I join him, pulling out seats for ourselves.

"I shall sit here 'til tomorrow," Henri complained to himself. "Or the next day, maybe."

"It's really dreadful," Alice mutters, "the way all these creatures argue. Violence hidden behind meaningless words. It's enough to drive one mad."

Henri nods along and finished his drink in two gulps.

We wait, watching the man who claimed he wanted to bring back someone from the dead practically ignore us.

"Are you going to drink that?" Henri suddenly asked.

I look to my drink. It's a very pale-yellow mixture with some bubbles and a lemon peel twisted over the rim of the glass. "What's mine is yours."

He flashes as smile, as if knowing he should when someone is flirting or allowing him something. But it's quickly lost as he takes the drink. This time he finishes it off even quicker.

Worried I'm missing something, I take Alice's drink. After a sip, I realize how not *quite* right I had been about the contents. It's lemonade alright, but it's also champagne, and a bit heavy on the gin. "I did not realize these were spiked."

"Oh." He blinked as if our table was coming into focus. "Can Alice not drink?"

"What? I don't know." The legal age for alcohol was, and likely would stay, the least of my concerns. "You're drinking like—"

"A fish?" He roughly finishes my sentence with his own pain.

I slowly shake my head. "Like you aren't having fun at this party."

"I outrank everyone here and yet I'm holding my father's table as if I was a child." Without asking, he takes the remaining drink. "I won't be able to have fun until I kill off these thoughts."

He at very least is babying the remaining flute of champaign. Eyes now back watching this father go on and on with some noble. Henri propped his chin up on his elbow. "We shall sit here for days."

"You're at least wanted here," Alice said, joining the pity party. "I'm just an extra who doesn't know much."

This simply won't do. There was no mirth here, so I'd have to create some. "Come play croquet with me."

"We were told to wait." Henri's words sound like a question, more than an objective fact.

"You'll never get out of this mood if you brood. Come on, the court is free right now. I'll even let you two have scramble against me."

Alice perked up, sitting a little straighter in her seat. "Our best shots against yours?"

I stand, taking a few steps backwards towards the court. "Come on, we were invited to play were we not?"

"Can we, please?" Alice adds. As Henri smiles, I know her words seals the deal.

Croquet is a simple game. The hardest part is that the balls must go in order, and I wasn't always best at linear things. I picked one of the mallets from the stand as Henri moved three balls toward the starting line.

"You start us off," he said. "We want to see what we are up against."

Alice beamed at the use of 'we' and nodded once in firm agreement. They were cute so I agreed and took the blue ball assuming the green was his.

I lined up the shot carefully. Since I didn't have to guess where the start was the ball passed perfectly through the first hoop. By the nature of the game, I went again until I missed right at the mouth of the fourth hoop.

Henri gestured for Alice to go next. She picked the

yellow ball and after a careful practice swing, she made it only past the first hoop. "Sorry," she mumbled as she returned to wait near the start.

"No worries," Henri said softly and took his turn. Hitting the ball consistently with the correct amount of force and distance to make it past the third hoop.

"We call next!" A deeper stray voice called. I glanced up to see a brutish man standing next to a twig of a woman.

I didn't want the game to end, but also planned on winning so keep going. Hitting the ball from the third to fourth, fourth to fifth, fifth to...

The ball stopped in line with the final hoop, but off to the left of it. *That's not what I meant to do.*

"You left us an opening," Henri said, clearly not as concerned with my missed shot as I was. Alice took her place. She was getting better already and got through two more hoops. Henri's next three shots however were the perfect trio needed to win.

Alice politely clapped. "You did it!"

"We did it," he correctly softly.

"I... I didn't help."

"Sure, you did," he said, with an encouraging nod. "Knowing I had back up made me relax so I could play better."

"Oh, well then," Alice chewed on her bottom lip for a moment unsure of what to say. "Go us."

"You go first this time," Henri said, nodding over to the starting line. "I'll be your back up."

"Okay!" Alice scooped up our balls and rushed them towards the start.

Henri stepped next to me waiting for Alice to take her

turn. "Thanks, by the way."

"For what?" My words were nearly a pout as I stared at the patch of grass that made my ball go wayward. I always won at croquet. I could win if the balls were hedgehogs, and the mallets the heads of flamingos.

"For letting us win," he laughed.

"I didn't."

"Madison, you might fool Alice. But not me."

My reply got hung up in my mouth. Wanting to say I didn't once more. Say I never aimed to fool anymore. Complain about the terrain, or cite I needed more lemonade to be my best.

"Oh please, mind what you're doing!" Alice cried. We looked over to catch her jumping back as the same voice from before was now a whole person standing on the court. He had decided to play without waiting for us to finish and was whacking his ball hard enough that it was nearly catching air.

"If everyone minded their own business," the brute continued, turning his nose up. "The world would go round a deal faster than it does."

"Which would not be an advantage," Alice boldly said. "Just think of what it would do to the time. You see the world takes twenty-four hours to turn around on its axis."

"Speaking of axes," the man replied, "back talk again and it will be off with your head."

Alice glanced anxiously toward me, as Henri stepped forward putting himself between them.

"Brother," the Frog Prince said, as if the word was a warning. "Mind your manners when speaking to my guests."

"By the stars, Francis," another woman said, as she

joined our group. It isn't the twig of the person who had been standing with him earlier. This woman looks their ages combined and walks with an air that she owns the place.

"What are you wearing?" Her hand reaches to mess with an ascot around Francis' neck and laughs to herself. "Wherever did you find this gaudy pattern?"

Henri had given his brother pause; this woman had shut him down completely. His eyes adverted as he started to mumble. "I thought you might like it. It's imported."

"Clearly some things should stay where they are from." Her hand slips away, as she moved towards Henri. He gains a hesitant smile as they kiss each other's cheeks, and she continues. "I'm sorry I was sleeping when you arrived."

"Completely understandable, Mother. We came in late," Henri starts, and waved us closer. "May I introduce you to Madison?"

She turned to me next, and I try not to look overly eager. Maybe someone who married into the Hart family wouldn't be as bad as the rest. The woman smiles, and I find myself mirroring it. "Did you know that my son hasn't brought any men back home?"

My grin grows a bit lopsided. "No, Madame Hart."

"He's a mage," Henri corrected.

"So are you," she said, tone clear that this is meant as a negative trait. Rather than something powerfully wonderous.

"No, I meant he is here for a spell Father wants."

"Oh." Her eyes don't catch my face again.

My heart sinks a little as I fall in her mental rankings. Briefly reaching the heights of 'possibly worthy of her son' before crashing into ranks of 'the help'. *Fucking bourgeois.*

She hummed a sigh. "Here I was hoping you'd finally brought someone you wanted my approval to marry."

"Anna, love," Pollux said, even though this conversation is devoid of any. "May I speak to Henri and his guests alone?"

She nodded and went to play croquet with her other son.

We walk a short distance away from the party. Around a path with circular step stones placed within the grass. "I told you to wait for me at the table," Pollux scolded.

"Alice wanted to play," Henri replied, "I couldn't say no to a Lady."

Pollux looked towards Alice, having forgotten about her. "Ah, right you were then."

No wonder Henri started drinking. My own patience was too dry for this. "I can't bring back the Queen of Hearts." *Wouldn't if could either, so there.*

"We will give you anything you want," Pollux offered as if he could hear my thoughts.

"What I want, you can't give." I start, and quickly decide that isn't everything I wanted to say. "She's been dead for months. A new ruler has even been chosen. Moving on would be the correct course."

"You don't understand—"

"I understand necromancy," I said, cutting him off. "Do you even have her body? If I had the body, the best I could do is bring back a hollow hungry thing. She wouldn't be fit to rule."

"My sister always had an appetite for power," he mused, being utterly useless. "I will find the body. And then we will discuss this more. Good day."

Pollux continues walking, as Henri stops following. The Prince just stands shaking his head. "I'm sorry. I'd be sorrier if I thought either of you were under the impression that manners here today were more than posturing."

Alice's weight shifts on her feet. "Does this mean we can go now?"

"Don't leave." Henri's outburst seemed to even surprise him. "It really doesn't matter what we do for the rest of the day. But it's considered rude to leave before the party officially ends tonight."

"I am allowed to drink by the way," Alice added, making her vote on the matter clear.

"Wonderland doesn't have such laws anyway, dear." Henri added, before they both waited for me to chime in with my answer.

"Fine. But only if I can make the party livelier."

"Oh, please do." Henri's tone is far too near the beg that he should have just started with.

Chapter Twenty

"**This** game is called King's cup," I decreed to the sitting group in front of me. The company tonight was comprised of every interesting person who came to the Hart's social event. Everyone else was already busy doing their own things. Or deeply vexed me.

There was the twig of a woman, Sarah. In my opinion, I saved her from Francis. She seemed to agree, and her biggest surprise was I wanted her for a drinking game instead of the private suggestions Francis had been propositioning.

The Duchess's daughter, Gemma was also here. I think she fancied Alice's commentary, but possibly other things.

There was a total of four men, including Henri and myself. He had just be on this side of sober all day. And the other men were chosen since they had been drinking 'lemonade' without ever making an ass of themselves.

"Each of us has a drink, and we will let the deck decide our fate," I said, dealing out everyone a face down card.

Alice looked the most nervous, having decided she didn't really like drinking, but would if it was part of a game. The 'rewards' in this would probably be flipped for her.

"Once all kings have been dealt the person who pulled the last one has to down everything from this large golden chalice I took from the front room," I explained. "Any questions?"

"How does that cup get filled?" Gemma asked, from her spot next to Alice.

"If you get one of the first three kings, you pour your existing drink in there," Alice said, looking at Gemma for a moment, before glancing towards me. "Right?"

"Exactly." However, Alice would need to keep her eyes on that jewel of a person if she wanted to win any related prizes. Gemma held herself with enough style, grace, and softness that I thought Alice might find value there.

"And no one peek at their cards," I added, and glanced over everyone who seemed ready. "I'll start."

When I flipped over the card it was a seven. "Heaven rhymes with seven. Whoever draws the next one gets paired up."

Henri stared intently down at his card, and I wished I knew if he was willing it to match or be any other number. Sarah playfully bumped her shoulder into him. "It's your go."

Henri flipped over a Jack of Hearts. "What does this one mean?"

"Whoever is dealt a Jack makes a new rule we all have to follow."

Henri frowned. "I thought dealer makes the rules."

"Only fair, it is your kingdom," I conceded.

"My rule is… no titles." He declared while looking down, then sternly over the people gathered. "No more titles tonight. If I hear one duchess, one prince, duke, any of it. You drink."

A brilliant rule, that made me wish I had caught the other men's names. But, oh well, hadn't needed them yet.

Sarah went next, flipping over a Jack of a different suit. "I want the next one to… declare what they deem sexy about the person next to them."

Gemma leaned in. "Next card, or next one?"

"Number one," Sarah clarified.

I found it curious that Sarah was sitting next to both her and Henri but said nothing as Gemma went. The next few people pulled cards that made them either drink or pour into the shared cup until the turn reached Henri again.

He pulled the One of Hearts, and again stared down at the card cautiously.

"Tell us, Prince Henri," Sarah giggled. "What do you find sexy about Madison?"

She didn't pick herself after all.

"Drink," Henri harshly said.

"What? Oh shoot, I said a title. Sorry!" She took a large drink from her cup.

Henri met my gaze and held it until there was a faint smile. "His eyes."

Can't say I expected that either, and clearly neither had Sarah since she scuffed. "You can look lower than his nose, Henri. We all have eyes. I'd say… his chest."

"Chest?" Alice asked, possibly thinking we all had those as well.

Sarah nodded. "Don't you just want to undo those shirt buttons? See what's underneath."

"Not particularly," the man to my right joked.

"Thank you, Sarah," I said, taking a drink as if that had been her proper title.

"Two rhymes with you," I explained as Alice turned over a black two. She picked Gemma to drink who seemed happy to do so.

"Six is dicks!" The guy next to her said as he flipped his card. "That means the men drink." The guy next to him lifted his cup and reached for his own card without delay.

"You don't know who among us have one," I said, lifting my cup all the same. "But I understand your intent."

The next two cards where three for 'me' and we drank until Henri flipped over the second seven.

Gemma instantly gasped. "Are you going to kiss?"

"It isn't Heaven if there's an unwanted audience." I glanced around the room. There was a cabinet but doubted it could hold one person let alone two.

"Go into the hallway," Gemma suggested.

Liking that idea, I stood, and offered my hand to help Henri up. "You game?"

"Dealer makes the rules." He took my hand, dropping it once he was up, and headed out to the hallway.

"Alice is the new dealer; we will be back in seven."

Henri was leaned against a wall, watching as I closed to door behind me. "I didn't expected to kiss you based on a random card flip."

"It wasn't random. I was creatively dealing so I could get you out of there."

He squeaked out a single syllable before laughing. "That actually makes more sense. Us getting the sevens, Alice getting cards where she doesn't have to drink."

"Do you approve?"

He pushed off the wall, placing himself a step closer. "I approve."

"Need to ask though," I said, licking my lips. "How *did* you expect to kiss me?"

Henri eyes were definitely looking below my nose this time. "Don't tease me. Especially not somewhere anyone could walk by."

"Shall we go somewhere private then?"

He laughed again. Soft and too short of a sound. "You don't stop, do you?"

"Not generally, no." I took a step closer, being as close as we could while still having air between us.

"We left our drinks behind." His voice lowered to account for the lack of distance.

"Would you like to go back?"

"No." His voice trailed off, and I thought he might close the remaining gap between us. "Let's sneak into the wine cellar."

Maybe time *was* on my side, since Henri was just buzzed enough that his inhibitions were gone, but not so removed from himself that I'd worry.

The only other company down here were the smooth

racks of redwood build into the walls of this almost damp cellar. There were no guards posted, but Henri still had to use some sort of sliding combo to open to door.

A polished stone tasting table was near the door with a decanter and glasses already laid out. A bottle was in a bucket for ice, but only water remained. It was possible someone was here yesterday, or even earlier for a tasting and simply hadn't finished the bottle off. The glasses looked clean so clearly they hadn't left in a rush.

"Are we allowed down here?"

"It is my kingdom after all," Henri mused, but the tone lost all humor. "My crown's actually here, in the house."

"Truly? Why?"

"Like you said… so my parents can play pretend."

"Do they wear it?"

Henri shook his head. "No, it's in the hall of records. Sitting there like a table center piece."

"That simply won't do." The golden cup for our drinking game had been taken, I could lift the crown too. That would have to wait, however. I had a more important thought after spending time with his parents.

"Hey, were you trying to protect me from your family with the handkerchief? You knew exactly what they'd complain about. Or skip over."

Henri's footsteps echoed within the tighter spaces of the cellar as he walked through the wine racks.

"At first," I continued, raising my voice a little as he went. "I thought you didn't want me to embarrass you. But, and I hate to say it, they don't seem to respect you much in the first place."

"It was probably a bit of both actually," he sighed,

placing back a bottle he was he was inspecting. "I know their opinion of me isn't going to change. I'm someone's son, and that's my use. But you don't deserve their nettling."

"That would be sweet if it wasn't so tragic."

"Many things are."

As if to test this theory, he stepped close. Eyes checking for permission before he pressed his soft lips against mine. My gasp of an inhale allowed his lips to melt even more into mine.

His hands rose to my arms, squeezing even as he pulls back a little. Still close enough that I rubbed my nose against his, hoping to catch his mouth again.

"I'm glad you're here," Henri whispered. "I think I'd lost myself if you weren't."

"I never lose anything." My hand cupped his cheek. "Usually the one collecting lost things actually."

"Madison." My name sounded like a plea. "I'm serious. Thank you for sticking around with me. *For* me."

"You're worth it."

He rolled his eyes and pulled further away. I let him go, watching as his arms stretch out wide as he turns in a circle. "Can you find me your birth year?"

"You're verging on drunk."

"Which means I'm not now. Come on. If you don't, I'm going to guess. Don't make me be accidentally rude in the attempt."

This seemed like an easy enough indulgence, so I go to the closest rack to check the years. Takes two bottles for me to figure out the newest bottles are in the front, so I venture around the corner to keep looking.

To my surprise, I find one and bring it back to Henri

who had walked halfway towards me already.

His eyes flare wider as he took the weight from my hand, clearing more dust off with his own fingerprints. "Wow, you must be the oldest person alive."

"Well…" I grin. "Not consecutively."

Not seeming to care about any math I might have to offer, he reached for the same buttons mentioned earlier on my shirt. I catch his mouth with mine, as his attempt to undress me fumbles a bit now that we are both distracted.

Far too soon, he steps back. Almost bumping into the bottles behind him. Brow furled and looking suddenly serious. "I have something I need to tell you."

"You can tell me anything."

His eyes are dilated, smoldering with intensity. A clear desire, that's being barely held off. "I'm, uh—my reputation for kissing has been oversold."

I found myself quite pleased with his work, so what did it matter? This doesn't seem all that important of a thought, so I pull him back by the hand. There's no resistance as I kiss his neck starting at the pulse point. "Reputations usually are exaggerated," I mumbled against his hot skin as I work my way down.

"Madison…"

If it were possible to be inebriated on another's voice, I'd be the drunk one. "I'm listening."

"I've never slept with anyone," he starts, and once he does the flood of words don't slow. "I've actually never done a lot of things. But once you're known for something people don't really let you change it. Only play into it.

The people who came to see me started to look at me with this… hunger. Like I was merely a well-reviewed tourist stop. I ended up wanting to hold on to *not* doing

135

things as if it had some value."

I'm not sure when I stopped working my mouth down his neck and pulled back to also show I was listening. But I had, as concern for him rooted deeper within me.

"And you… probably have experienced *everything*. Sure, I've kissed plenty. But… This probably all sounds so stupid. 'Virginity' is probably old fashioned." He turned his head away, staring at a decorative facing on the wall. "Shit, maybe I am like my family."

"Henri," I whisper, turning his face back to me. It was hard not to kiss him this time. "First off, you're not like them. Second, I like you. Full of experience or lacking it. Neither is a flaw."

His body was angled towards me, chest quickly raising and falling. Still grasping the unopened bottle. "Will you show me?"

Fuck.

My hands ached to touch him again. I wanted to pick him up and set him down on the wine tasting table. He was as drunk as he was beautiful. "I need something from you first."

"Anything."

Fuuck.

I was often the bad guy. A careless soul. But Henri deserved better then to have something like this bookended by his parent's bullshit.

"Finish this, if you want." I put my hand on the bottle, guiding both to his chest. "Because if you keep being so damn attractive my reservations aren't going to last much longer, and we both should be able to remember tonight."

Henri blinked down the bottle. "I can't open it here."

136

"I didn't mean right this second."

He ran a free hand through his hair and stepped to the side so he could walk past me towards the table. Next to the bucket was a bottle opener. He popped the cork and drank deeply. Wiping his mouth as I leaned across the other side of the table. "I just realized how embarrassed I am."

"I'm sorry," I said, trying not to grin. "It's cute on you though."

Henri blew out a breath, before taking another sig. A reasonable sized one this time at least. "Are you..." He looked over, and I wanted to know what he saw there. "Trying to make this special for me?"

I nodded. "Is it working?"

"Yeah." He kissed me again from cross the table and left my lips with a tart taste of wine. "I guess you really do believe in love."

I guess I did.

Chapter Twenty-One

Turns out we weren't the only ones who had spent the night drinking. Only the staff and I didn't seem to have a hangover.

A maid rushed around trying to clean everything as people dozed off their day of parting.

"Excuse me," I said, feeling guilty for putting myself in her busy path. "Can you tell me where the Halls of Records is?"

She didn't seem to want to tell me at first, but after a glance around at the mess decided not to add a delay by refusing. "Past the study, door on the right."

"Thank you." I moved out of her way, and she instantly resumed her frantic pace. The study had been thankfully easy to find, down the same hall that Henri and I stopped in last night. The cellar was also on the right, but past it was another door.

A Hall of Records, in my opinion should have been a storage area crammed with papers that proved lineage, land rights, and held a written history of everything.

Instead, there was wall to wall glass display cases. Every treasure was accompanied by a lit candle. The room itself would've felt large if wasn't for a sizeable wooden table in the middle.

There was no way it would have fit through the door. The table was standing height, to account for the lack of chairs around it. And in the center, just like Henri described, was a golden crown resting within a wirework bird nest.

I glanced back at the door, surprised this room wasn't guarded. Then again, this was the Hart's home and long past hosting hours. No one remaining was meant to ever consider thievery.

With both my hands out, I lifted the crown up. The weight of gold always surprised me. Like most, I found the shimmer captivating. Unlike most, to me its value wasn't monetary. Gold is ancient. Not a single new ounce had been created since time started in Wonderland.

I tilted my head forward so my top hat would fall onto the table. Then with as much reverence as one could have when dropping something, hid the crown away.

There were so many ways to go about giving this crown back to its rightful owner. I thought of wearing it and nothing else. Always a showstopper.

But it didn't feel right for this crown, or this person.

In our wing of the manor, Henri was with Alice on the patio. The smell of paint thinner was strong enough that I knew what they were up to this afternoon long before seeing them.

"Hey Madi," Alice said. A little wave followed as I approached before she turned back to study the canvas Henri was working on.

"She mentioned you were already awake," Henri said, with soft smile. They seemed so vibrant under the rising sun. "I should have believed her."

"I was out getting you something." My hand removed my hat and held it out like a present.

His eyes fell from me to the offering. Confused enough that he hadn't even put his brush down yet.

"It's inside."

Henri wiped his hands on the smock he had on. Then reached into the hat, and clearly misjudged its depth. Pausing to give a funny little expression, he sunk his arm in further in, reaching in up to his forearm.

His eyes were wide like what he was doing was impossible as he carefully pulled the crown out. "This… this is mine."

"Exactly."

A nervous exhale followed. "You stole this?"

"Consider it reclaiming." I took a step forward to look at his painting more clearly. The stroke style matched those back at his place. Well, except for the mismatched image of him. "I didn't know you had so many talents."

"Huh?" Henri briefly looked back towards the canvas before the weight of what was in his hand stole his attention again. Then he laughed. It was a small giggle that broke into a full joyous sounding thing. "You weren't actually meant to take this."

"Shall I put it back?"

My hands were folded together, but he leaned away as if I had reached for it. "No, it's mine."

"Now this is a scene worth painting," Alice decreed. Her hands were out, thumbs and index fingers touching to make a rectangle picture frame.

"Would you like to paint?" Henri asked me. "There's another easel and more canvas."

"I love painting." The words made me feel naughty somehow. Like I'd felt up the metaphorical crown jewels, instead of the literal ones.

"Yeah?" He asked brightly, and how I wanted to kiss him again. Alice seemed to be rooting for us, might even make the scene more picturesque.

"It may be a waste of supplies since my muscle memory gets reset every time I swap bodies." It was a completely insane sentence that both of them blessedly took in stride.

"If you love it, do it anyways." Alice got up and moved around to grab another canvas. Henri took this as his sign to prop up another stand.

"I don't paint," she continued as she offered a rolled bundle of brushes. "Because it's messy. The droplets get everywhere and stress me out."

Considering that, I moved the easel a little bit further out on the patio just in case when cleaning between colors it did indeed get messy.

As I picked up the brush, I could tell I wasn't holding it right. My muscles weren't matching what I knew it should feel like. The smallest details like this never stuck.

But all the same, we painted, joked, and hung out together until the sun shifted the lighting around. It must have been around dinner since Alice excused herself to get food.

"Can I see your hat?"

I glanced up from my painting to see Henri taking a step towards me. His own crown off, as if looking to swap it.

"Looking to roleplay each other?"

He smiled. "Sounds refreshing to be honest. Come on, indulge me again."

Yes, sir.

Instead of doing an imitation after we traded, he studied the curious hat. Reaching his hand in again to see if he could touch anything else. But the only thing he seemed to be able to do consistently was reach past the visual depth. "This is so wonderous."

I placed his crown on my head, not knowing really what to do with it, and mostly not wanting to hold while I continued to paint.

"What are you making?" He asked a moment later, stepping close enough now that I could smell the soap he must have used this morning.

"Something abstract."

He studied the botches of greens and blues. I had been painting via feeling rather than trying to make it be anything. "I think it says, 'You promised me a roleplay'."

"I did not." He grinned. If he kept smiling like that I'd volunteer as a court jester to be become the repeated cause.

"You're the one who said it would be refreshing."

He nodded slightly, expression growing a bit more somber. "You seem so… free."

"Then try me."

"What?" His face suddenly flushed. "Pretend I'm you?"

After an encouraging nod from me he went on.

"Okay, I'm the most powerful mage in all the lands, and I do silly things like touching things that belong to powerful households."

"Little on the noise," I coached, like our day painting had turned into an improv class. "Keep going. Why would I do silly things?"

Henri's eyes lifted to his crown. "Because you're standing in front of the Frog Prince."

When his lips parted I turned fully away from my painting, running my hand up his arm. Voice dropping to a whisper. "And what would this Prince like to do?"

His eyes fell to my lips, and I was unable to resist temptation a second longer. Henri swayed as we kissed like I was a tidal wave that would knock him down. My hand gripped a little tighter to steady us. It was a kiss worth drowning in.

Noises of people moving elsewhere in the house caused Henri pull away. I breathed in like I forgot for a moment that air was even a thing living things needed.

"I… We're going a little fast."

Understanding how was lost on me, but I knew when to back off. Henri glanced towards the door. I didn't see anyone there, but also knew when someone needed reassurance.

"I don't really age, so take your time."

Henri nervously pushed his hair back, making himself look even more freshly fucked. I knew that wasn't true, but oh how I wanted to make it true by teatime.

He seemed to relax when Alice returned. She looked at our swapped headpieces for a moment. "Aw, unfair. I want cool accessory."

At the same time, we both offer the other's. Her eyes

143

widen as if we'd ruled she could replace any meal with ice cream.

Alice put her food down, before accepting both from us. My top hat goes on first and she very carefully placed the crown on top. Sitting up properly to maintain the balance.

It seemed the secret to getting the Frog Prince's physical affections was just spending time with him. Because the third day after our wine cellar conversation, he was sprawled out on a chaise lounge waiting for me.

"I don't mean to criticize," Henri said, "but I'm pretty sure I'm meant to be naked."

It was a hilarious statement and warranted a laugh first and foremost. "I already told you what you're supposed to do."

"It's just…" His nose squished up, making all sorts of wrinkles. "Explaining my sexual hang ups isn't that sexy."

I sat back on my heels on the floor below him. "This isn't to rehabilitate your fears. I'd like to know them as a boundary to make sure they get excluded. That way everything that we do is enjoyable."

Henri held a hand to his mouth considering. "What's yours?"

Well, he was right about one thing. This part wasn't sexy. My thoughts rather just rush past. But fair is fair.

"Being trapped," I start and don't want to leave it without the why. "Sex makes me feel the most alive, most grounded in my own body. But I worry about feeling stuck somewhere like there's nowhere left go."

Henri sat up on his forearms listening with a concerned little expression. "Wow, shit. Now I really must tell you mine now, huh?"

He slowly and deeply inhaled. "Okay. Seems silly in comparison, but I'm afraid things will hurt. And that... someone will hear, and the moment won't only be ours anymore."

"It's not silly. Thank you." I moved to kneel on the lounge by his feet. "Do you trust me?"

Henri bit his lip, and it slips out under his teeth. "More than ever."

"I want to worship every inch of you." My hand starts to trail up his leg as I crawl over him and stop to hover my mouth over his.

"The nobility isn't worth your admiration," he said, craning his head up, but can't quite reach me. And damn, did he say the naughtiest little things.

"No, but you are." Any reply turned into a moan under my lips. And I'm all too happy to please, anything in service of the kingdom. And Henri. Okay, exclusively Henri.

One hand was needed to hold me up, but the other held the side of his face. A slight tremor in my fingers highlighted its own eagerness. Then broke the kiss so I could run my fingers over his flush plump lips.

His tongue darted out to lick my finger as I moved my mouth to trail down his neck. Henri tilted his head back allowing me to kiss and nibble to my content.

My hand slid lower over his chest. Finding a hint of skin before hitting fabric. My fingers balled the shirt up. "Can I ruin this?"

"Uh huh," he breathed out.

I sat back, so I'd be able to grip the poet shirt from each

side of the v neck and ripped it past the navel until where it was tucked into his pants.

"Aggressive," Henri said, near purr.

He started to sit up, but my hand touched bare skin, gently holding him down as his breathing picked up the pace. "Have patience."

I slid the ripped shirt off his shoulders. It remained beautifully draped around the rest of him, framing his hips as the fabric stayed gathered at the waist against contrasting skin. The romantics wouldn't be able to capture the awe of it all.

Henri's hands reached for me, one coming to rest along my hipbone. While I turned my hand to hold the other. Drawing it up to my mouth and kissing along his wrist, before sliding my mouth over his knuckles and over his fingertips.

He let out a quiet whine before speaking. "Please take care of the rest of these clothes next."

I pulled my hand free, and his fell away on its own. Pretending I didn't know what he meant, I reached for his crotch. Putting pressure on an area that was already tighter than when we started. "These clothes?"

"Y—"

At the first sound of the word, I rocked my hand over his length. Pressing my advantage without apology, as his words hitched with a small wave of pleasure.

"All of them, Mads."

"Ask nicely," I teased, brushing my fingers over his stomach as if he was a canvas.

His eyes fluttered at the feather light touch. "Maybe I want to be mean."

My insides started to feel like a warm puddle with his words alone. My hands worked their way down his pants. One finger dipping under unable to wait to feel the soft skin there. "Ooo, do you now?"

"F-Fucking," he gasped, pledged. "Don't make me beg."

"As you wish." All the mock fumbling around allowed for quick access when I really wanted. With his cock cradled in my hand I started to work it. I wanted to introduce every different act as something that could be full of joy and ecstasy. A first that the felt comfortably and deeply on equal footing.

Henri arched his back, body rutting towards me, heat growing. Looked too blissful to complain about anything as long as I didn't stop.

A fact proven by his whimper as I stopped for a moment to take off my own shirt. When I started again it was at a steadily increasing the rhythm.

Henri moaned louder, hands looking for purchase against the lounge but didn't even have sheets to grab. "Oh fu—*God!*"

That was a rare cuss. One usually reserved for those actively hoping for some magical guardian. He looked unmoored, and not in a completely pleasured way.

I gave him a second and grabbed my shirt. "Here, open your mouth."

He blinked but obeyed, and I put my shirt between his teeth to muffle all his future obscenities. "You good?"

Henri bit down, mumbled an agreement into the wad of fabric. His eyes gleamed, eager for me to continue. My mouth moved to lick across salty skin, as my hands now shared work was becoming easier with a hint of slickness.

"Come for me," I whispered in his ear. As if those were

magical words, pleasure took over as he both tensed and twitched. A muffled moan followed as warmth spilled free in my hand.

He spit out my shirt, panting for a few breaths. Then grabbed my face and anchored my lips to his.

I sighed contently from the intensity of the shared moment. Dying wasn't in my nature, and there might be no greater celebration of being alive—and together.

Chapter Twenty-Two

Breakfast was the most important meal of the day. Let it be known across the land, because I was being feed a forkful of pancake by someone I cared about. It didn't bother me that he was a prince either. I decided Henri could be the exception to anything he wanted.

Alice was next to us at the table. Since I didn't need to eat, she and Henri were working on finishing the third plate that had been brought out to us.

"Try the bacon," Henri said, lifting a piece. Not giving a single fuck as he kept it suggestively just far enough to make me lean into his space for it.

"*Mmm,* that's actually ready good." I took a moment to savor it before shallowing. "Compliments to the chef. And pig."

Anna cleared her throat in a not-so-subtle way to get us to stop. I glanced over to the sound; Henri's mother was still eating her breakfast in bird sized bites. While Pollux sat there with a full plate. I think we ruined his appetite. *Oops.*

"How are the lands these days, son?" Anna asked. "It's dreadful that I never get to visit any of the kingdoms unless they come see me. Has the Beast found a beauty?"

"Still mourning the last," I answer.

As she sits back in her seat in surprise, I realize the topic was not meant to be an open discussion.

Anna offers a polite smile before continuing on. "And who is the other princess I'm thinking of? The faraway one? Oh, Henri, you always remember her name."

"Jasmine, Mother."

"Ah yes." She smiles a bit brighter. "Have you spoken with her recently?"

"Not since the last vote." Henri speaks around his breakfast, but the disinterest in the conversation is going ignored.

"We'll find a suitable match for you," Anna starts properly distanced between bites. "Since that's what you've been playing at this whole time. Simply let your family help."

Henri's jaw tightens. "Of course, Mother."

Alice sputters. As she looked over at me, I shake my head slightly to discourage whatever thought is there. She covers by taking a sip of water.

Henri's hands reach under the table to sit on his lap. Waiting only a moment before one moved over to my knee to give it a squeeze in silent thanks.

Pollux is now pushing food around his plate as if breakfast is an annoying formality rather than something needed to sustain yourself.

"Father, you are the one who invited us this morning," Henri said, finishing off his pancakes before continuing. "If this was pretext, then just... out with it."

"Why, I never!" Pollux's raised voice and stumble for the next words are met with a hushing sound from his wife. He looks over as if further betrayed.

"You are the one who wanted Henri and his friends to stay here this whole past week." Anna turns a kinder expression towards us. "No offense implied, dear. I love having you here."

She was still very clearly talking to only Henri. But whatever, since I actually only cared about her son's approval, so bygones and what not.

"None taken, Mother." Henri smiled. "I agree with Madison though."

His father glared. *Shit, what had I said?*

"Compliments to the chef."

"And the pig," Alice dared.

Pollux threw his napkin onto his meal. "If you must be so perverse about death and force my hand, then fine. I haven't found Cassandra's body yet."

"What a shame," I said sounding my part, but not really meaning it. I had eyes for the rest of the bacon on Henri's plate. The pig had been renamed in this form making death already at the table.

"I have another idea," Pollux said, through gritted teeth.

I spit out my stolen bacon onto my plate. Even something of this quality could be suddenly soured by whatever his next idea would be.

We were brought into a study with several books already laid out on the table. It was odd enough was that they looked larger than any other of the untouched tomes in this room, but more curious however was we hadn't entered an empty room.

There was already a mage standing in front of the books. A hand was perched near his mouth, leather gloves unevenly cut to allow his fingers to be free. It was hard to look directly at him since the smell that wafted off was rank. Less of death, and more of broken boundaries.

Pollux moved to the other side of the table, looking down at the books and not seeming to notice anything strange. Henri seemed a bit standoffish, pausing by the door, but there wasn't a tell as to why.

"Your idea came from a book?" Alice craned her head over, but as soon she took a step closer to the stranger slid the book further away.

Pollux turned up his noise at her. "What an ignorant girl you are."

"I'm an adult, who has grown out of caring about what those who speak ill of me say." Alice puffed out her chest. As if to prove her claim, she moved closer to look again. "It's a spell book."

"Where did you get it, Father?" Henri asked softly, from behind me and the room felt a mite small for all of us.

"I secured it from the Queen's winter castle," Pollux said, effortlessly for the amount of falsehood in his words.

"You mean the Wolf King's college," I corrected. When it was the Queen's winter castle, all of the books were hidden away from the public so only she could control who learned magic. Malcolm's goal had been to change that. Give the knowledge to any hurting soul who needed it. "What did you do to the school?"

"Nothing." Pollux raised a hand like I was cruel to even accuse him. "Milo here simply took a book that was offered. Surely you can't steal from someone who is freely giving knowledge."

It was a good thing we had left the room with the knives

because my urge to stab him was quickly raising.

None of us said anything else, and Pollux smiled as if that's exactly how we all should be. "You see as talented as Milo is with magic, he isn't your friend."

Who and what Pollux is talking about was getting harder for me to follow. Henri stepped forward as if summoned directly, so I opted to just watch.

Pollux rewarded his son by putting a hand on his shoulder. "I couldn't find your aunt, but you can still help our family get back what was lost."

"How?"

"This is for a séance," Milo explained.

I moved forward to look, but he still does not budge. So, I not-so-politely nudge him over a step so I can read the text. My hands recoil from the book once I understand what it actually is.

"What's wrong, Madi?" Alice asked, seemingly the only person caring about my reaction. Milo refills the void as I step further back towards her. Henri and his father continue to look down at the book. "What does the spell do?"

"It's not a séance, it's a *living possession.*"

Pollux's gaze is on his son now. Tone soft, just above a whisper. "I know you've been distracted by this…" His hand lifts vaguely in my direction. "Queer new thing. But whatever strange charm this Mad Hatter has will wear off."

"Father…"

"Your family needs you. Cassandra needs you. I need you, Henri."

His eyes are fixed on the ground, seemingly unable to even rise his head under Pollux's gaze.

"Alice," I breath out, needing at least someone to hear

and acknowledge me. "The Hart's are assimilationists. The dying accent and land are all they have left. When the Queen of Hearts ruled the reins of fate were still in their family's hands. But they gave up their culture to value their blood line. One that doesn't even have the crown any longer."

"How pitiful," Alice added, with a daring amount of understanding beneath those two words.

Pollux however did not take this summary of his family as kindly. Sneering at me as he spoke. "What is culture if not a bloodline?"

"*A soul.*"

"You're still wrong, Hatter," Pollux said, chin turned up as if he could finally smell his own bullshit.

"How so?"

"We still have a crown." His hand grips tighter on his son's shoulder.

A cold sweat breaks out as if my body knew his meaning before even my mind did. "Henri."

The name is a mere whisper on my lips, but Pollux nods. "If this doesn't work. If you refuse to do the spell allowing me to talk to my sister once more. I'll simply arrange a marriage, and we will ascend to the throne once more. As distracted as he has been with suitors, he is part of this family first and foremost."

My mouth fails to catch any words, and I'm even more concerned that Henri is allowing someone to speak of him like breedable livestock. If he couldn't defend himself, it would become difficult to remain an uncaring thing.

"Maybe I shall marry him off to your Alice," Pollux dared, drunk of his own assumed power. "Surely someone not from our land has the air of divinity."

Alice steps back, as I round the table and advance on

him.

"Your will be done? Do you think that makes you a god in this tale?" I didn't need necromancy to finish off his pitiful soul. With a shove, I separate him from his son.

Pollux stumbles back towards a bookshelf, and I grab his throat and start squeezing. The anger gave me plenty of room to breathe. Creates a buffer between me and a fate I'd never allow happen. "Because I've never come across anything I couldn't kill."

Milo moves to defend his patron, but it takes nothing more than a raised hand to hold him off. Without a touch, Milo starts making his own choking sound. His hands quaking as they rise to his ears. Droplets of blood start to pool there as if all the stolen knowledge is now leaking out towards freedom.

"Madison, leave my father be."

Listening wasn't on my to do list right now. The fact that those were Henri's first words while he had been silent the whole time his and Alice's freedom had been threatened only fueled my rage. *Silence until now.* In defense of an awful man that could so easily be snuffed out. How many others would have a better life if this one ended?

"Are you a murder, Hatter?" Henri moved into my line of sight, taking a very visual stance over whose side he was on. "Stop killing him."

I was more offended by him using the title than the insinuation of anything else. "Fine," I said, biting down on the word and letting my anger slip away. Leaving the room entirely as Henri stayed to tend to his father.

Chapter Twenty-Three

"Madison, wait."

I wished the voice belonged to Henri, but it was Alice's as she sprinted to catch up to me. I stopped and waited because I didn't even know where I was going. This whole place was stupidity theirs.

"The Prince asked me to make sure you didn't leave."

"Did he now?" Maybe I should have been thankful, but her tone suggested I was meant to stay as a necromancer. As the Mad Hatter. Not as Henri's personal guest. That was Alice's title. "I'm not in the mood for company, so you should keep yourself busy with something else."

"I don't want to leave. I'm here for you, Madi."

"Oh." My words weren't enough for this little ray of sun that was following me around, but I didn't know what to say either. So, my hand awkwardly patted the top of her golden head. Alice pawed my hand away with a smile.

On the way back to the rooms we'd been given, we crossed through a grand ballroom with gold crown molding.

Alice stopped as her eyes climbed up the six finished layers it made up. "This is their legacy, huh?"

Cassandra's molding, the seventh, was still tacky. Large blank panels sat empty where her most proud moments from her reign would have gone if she hadn't been murdered.

Does one mourn all crime, or simply call it justice for deeds that went unpunished?

Alice sighs up at it. "Their story sure is important to them."

I nodded. "And only theirs."

Alice glanced over to me. "Would you like some tea?"

"There's always time for tea."

Having a body was great when you knew how to make it feel different things. Most had to guess what would make them feel better. Not me. Not with potions.

Alice and I had our teatime in Henri's room. Figuring if he wanted us around it's where he'd eventually return. A theory I started to doubt now that I was lying on his bed, exceptionally high, and looking up at my refection in the mirrors above his bed and scrying.

My company had excused herself some time ago. Telling me to stay put as she wondered off somewhere or other. Didn't matter if she wasn't here because I was only half here myself.

Floating around my reflected image was glimpses of Wonderland. With a wave of my hands the image would change as if looking for something better.

The Frog Prince's crown was cradled on silk sheets. I had been playing around, placing it on Henri's head in jest, only for it to slide off without care as he straddled me. Royally riding me in the best and most literal way.

His skin was warm like the sun filled afternoon anywhere he touched. My hands squeezed his thighs soaking in the extra heat in my cold bones.

This… By every star in the sky was what I had wanted. I felt tension in every muscle just wanting to dissociate further into this possible timeline.

I had to stay lucid. This wasn't a thread I was meant to follow. Least not yet. And it would never happen if we didn't make up. Or maybe this was meant to be something that I had missed. Either way, I didn't want to see it anymore.

While skimming the threads of the magical tapestry that made the reflection, a rune filled my vision. Its brightness flooded everything else out as it had a story to tell.

"Sir," a voice started to apologize. "I'm unable to perform this spell."

"What do you mean *un*able?" Pollux said, his voice far too familiar to my ears. "Milo, you are paid to do as I say."

"I know, I'm sorry." The rune dimmed my eyes adjusted. His fingerless gloves were pulled off as the symbol burned into the leather. "I can't summon the dead. I'm not a necromancer."

"Keep trying."

I continued to watch the piece of time that was playing the past above me. Smoke filled within the surface. Swirling freely at first until it built and pushed against the glass.

There was a cry of anguish, a whine just barely this side

of human. Something was being summoned. Another almost nearly forgotten form of magic.

"I need more power," Milo hissed towards a man on all four beneath in. His body was aglow with similar and different runes. Hair covered his eyes and looking like he was going lose himself to pain. But I knew this man.

"The Wolf King," I said, with no other emotion besides recognition. A howl came from the portal Milo summoned behind Malcolm as if to confirm the truth.

The runes that I had seem burnt into Mal's skin connected him to the summoner's call like letters gathering to form specific words.

This once and tired king mumbled something through the strain and weight of it all.

Milo leaned in closer to listen. "What was that?"

"You want more power?" Malcolm lifted his head up to glare into the summoner's eyes. *"Make it yourself."*

"Madison, sober up right this second!"

Alice's voice made me tense up. Visions of the past slipped from me as my head turned towards her voice.

She was standing at the foot of the bed with her hands on her hips. After images of Alice moved about showing different places she might have gone, or still might go, as the Alice in this moment of time stayed still.

"You promised Claudia you'd help me."

"Not in this second." The after images stirred to cover a wider range of emotions. Mostly anger, but it was hard to tell without feeling any myself right now. One of the false-Alices threw a pillow across the room, so it seemed fitting to assume.

"Look, if you feel unsafe, just have some more tea. It's

what keeping my own murderous intent at bay."

"I didn't ask you to be tame," Alice said, "I want you to rescue the rabbits."

I sat up, looking at her more carefully as the colors flexed and wobbled. A red string looped around her wrist surely to somewhere she wished to return. "What rabbits?"

"I was killing time and found out that the Duchess has a bunch of rabbits in cages. They aren't pets, they are those white messenger rabbits."

"We mustn't do that. Are you sure?"

"I'm fairly sure. How many wild rabbits do you know carry little scrolls in little bags?

"No, I believe you. I meant kill time." All of translucent colored Alices narrowed into just this Alice as I stood. "Let's follow this web you've got wound up in."

"I don't know what that means but thank you."

Alice bought us outside, past the stables, and towards a small chicken coop.

"Wait!" I stopped suddenly in the middle of a cart path between where we were and where she was going.

The magical string around Alice's wrist snagged as she turned towards me. "What? What's wrong now?"

Now. What a funny little word. It wasn't wrong just now; it bad been wrong then. "Is the Wolf King okay?"

"What?"

Right, right, she hadn't been scrying with me. Did not witness the history I had. He still had that coin. "Never mind. We need to work on your current problem."

Her smile held a degree of concern, but she dashed ahead to make up for the time lost. Then ducked low, below the windows of the chicken coop. "Take a peek inside."

The smell of straw, dusty feed, and feces had been growing as we approached, but was quite strong pressed this close. Wood framing and chicken wire created the closure within. But the collection of chickens had been replaced with an assortment of rabbits. If cages had any merit in the first place, it didn't matter since the animals were too large for their enclosure.

Well, that was sobering sight that could knock you on your ass. "How do you know it was the Duchess?"

"She was tending to them before I came back to get you." Alice peered in, nose basically resting on the windowsill. "I don't think she keeps them forever. Delays them maybe? The Duchess released one when I was watching the first time."

"No wonder they are always late."

"Can we free them?"

"Absolutely." A heavy layer of wood shavings covered the wooden floor making sure they couldn't dig themselves free. But thankfully saw no other unlucky feet, besides theirs. "I don't see anyone, you?"

"No, let's do this quick." Alice moved to the door that was meant to keep chickens in during the night. Once inside, she didn't seem to have any idea what to do besides twisting wire back in an attempt to unlock each cage. "Why would anyone do this?"

"There must be profit in it somehow." Sustainable living was admirable, but it was clear the manor's eggs did not come from here.

"You seem oddly calm about this. I'd thought you'd be more upset given the shops seem special to you."

"They are." I began working on freeing rabbits along the

other side. As they started to hop around our feet it was becoming tricky to crouch down enough without stepping on the almost free rabbits. As I pulled back a makeshift cage door one of the barb wires caught my palm. Just like these rabbits, my paws didn't have padding either as I had to pull the wire back out from between my fingers. Probably mortifying usually, but that was the perk about this moment. "I don't feel a lot right now. I don't think my pain receptors are even firing."

"What? Geez!" Alice looked at my hand, ready to drop what she was working on to cater to it. "You must be more careful with yourself."

I pressed my lips together, not knowing how to explain that this *was* me being careful. The jab was barely bleeding, and seeing my own blood was surprising common. "Not to worry, all things pass."

"You should get a tetanus vaccine. Does this place have those?"

"I haven't the faintest idea of what you just said, so I'm going with no." What I did know is that it was wrong for these creatures to be locked up, which was enough for me right now.

We freed the last one, and the rabbits gathered inside finally started hopping out the door towards freedom.

"Coast is still clear," Alice declared. I secured the chicken coop's door behind me in hopes no one would notice anything happened until they came to directly look.

We snuck back to Henri's room. Opting to climb over the patio banister instead of using any proper entrance.

"Goodness, there you are," Henri said, rising from his seat.

"Don't be sour that we took a walk." I quickly folded my hands behind my back, so he didn't have any prompt to ask where we had been.

"I'm not."

My eyes lifted to his face. Expression soft once more. *Oh*, he really wasn't being rude. "Miss us then?"

"I feared you left." Henri instinctively stepped closer before catching himself. "I talked to my father more."

Whatever pull I had been feeling return snapped harshly back on me. My tea was wearing off and I was starting to feel things again. Everything was regaining an emotional charge. "I'm not interested."

"You brought us here to convince them to not go through with this plan," Alice said, blessing me with some back up.

"That's when I thought an animated corpse would sit on the highest throne. One measly séance will take no more than a single afternoon."

I wondered whose words were being used. His, or his elders. The answer was soon revealed when his tactics changed. "You owe me for almost killing my father."

"Like shit I do." I wish people understood the freedom that came with long outliving anyone who had once controlled you. Parents, or otherwise. I glanced to Alice who unfortunately did not seem to have me on this one.

"It's this," Henri started, "or I'll have to marry."

Henri should have just picked up a knife and stabbed it into my heart. That would have been an easier wound to heal. "I thought we were something."

"I owe my family at least this. Just one more thing," he started quietly. "Let me help them." He stepped forward, looking eager like he'd have scooped my hands up if I hadn't held them back. "The Queen of Hearts is dead. What more harm could she do?"

"Dead things can do all sorts of harm."

"But you'd be the one in control of it, therefore it will be safe. Please, for me."

This logic unfortunately had a bit of merit. "I need to think about it. Please rethink the whole situation as well."

"I'll await your answer."

With a growing annoyance it was becoming clear that we were all waiting on me. I sat stewing even as they fell sleep. Milo was a summoner, not a necromancer. It wasn't even the same medium of art.

Furthermore, summoners were meant to go on pilgrimages, gain the willing support of whatever they summoned. Not just rip people from wherever they were, angry and in pain. That twisted mage mustn't be allowed to exploit Henri too.

He stirred softly, being careful not to disturb Alice who was sleeping on top of the comforter. Without another word, just a rub of his eyes, he got up and set out three cups.

Curious. I moved closer to watch him better. The water smoked as he poured it from a pitcher that had been sitting out all night into a smaller container. Then he scooped something ground up into the water. A funny little lid was placed on top and pressed the sediment down.

"Here," Henri said, and poured me the first cup. "A cure for the morning monster inside us all."

A potion? I took the cup, gingerly taking a sip. It's too hot and bitter for tea and I realize it isn't. "Henri, this is coffee."

"Yeah," he smiled.

If only he would stop, I might be able to find myself able to say no. "Why am I still here if you've made up your mind about what's going to happen?"

"Because you're mine, Madison." He spoke calmly but ended up looking like he burnt his tongue on the words. Flushed from a truth he believed but hadn't meant to say.

I should have hated those words. But there was something exquisite about them. Not his Hatter, not his advantage at war, or a mad man. His ...*me*.

Henri's fingers tightened around the delicate cup. "I didn't mean to say that."

"Is that how you really feel?"

His mouth hung agape, tensing like I scolded him. "Yes."

I lowered my drink, and he mirrored the silent motion. Both of us watching, as my fingers hesitatingly covered his, doubting we'd touch.

"You are what I want the world to be," Henri continued, "Where people are undefined by the body they were born with. Free from anything and everything except what they choose to believe in. Possibly even endless."

His voice lifted above the near whispered exchange, enough that he glanced to see if he woke Alice. "I don't see things like you do. I have responsibilities. Maybe in time the world can be different. But this is the one we live in now."

"Please." My other hand reached across the table to catch him. "Let me show you the future. All of them. The ones with me and without. There's so many choices if you follow your heart."

"It's a matter of heart..." His voice sounded so different as he not quite repeated me.

"Henri, please don't ask this of me."

"I must do this. It's my duty, I'm sorry."

Chapter Twenty-Four

The only thing worse than showing up for this perverse ritual was knowing it was happening and not being there to keep an eye out on Henri.

Alice and I gathered things we could into a bag for supplies. It was a random assortment of whatever might be needed to safely pull off this harebrained idea.

We walked through the halls, stopping our militant march outside the set of double doors everyone had already gathered in. Listening for voices inside before diving straight in.

"The rabbits are gone," The Duchess said loud enough for anyone to overhear. Her business clearly not a secret to the family. "I'm not sure what happened."

"How strange," Pollux replied, quieter but still clear enough with some effort. "This will make our trade route times look worse."

Business! On a day like this…

Alice threw open the doors for us, striding in first like

we owned the place, and defiantly pulled her bag forward looking ready for anything.

Surprise washed over Henri's tired face. "You're here."

He was standing in the middle of the room. Family on one side, Milo on the other as if we had interrupted a hush hush wedding.

"Of course," I said, smiling softly. "I am your Madison."

His eyes burned with relief, making him look like he had woken up from a nightmare to good company. And I wished I could reassure him that it would be fine from here on out. But it wouldn't be.

Anger rose in me when I saw Milo still standing by. Jealousy wasn't the right word for it. The summoner had kissed boots and broken boundaries to get where he was. "If I sense a lick of your magic this afternoon, you'll be summoning your own death."

Milo started to roll his eyes as he held his hands up. Making a show of his step back towards a chair he does not end up sitting in. As long as he doesn't do magic, I could tolerate his existence.

"Yes, yes," Pollux scoffed. "You are very scary. Can we get along with it?"

Henri lowered himself onto his knees in front of me. Fairly sure that isn't what his father meant, but I'm personally loving the view.

"Do you need the book?" Alice asked. When I shake my head, feeling preoccupied with looking down into Henri's eyes, I'm glad she continues. "Gloves like discussed?"

"Yes, please."

Milo had been right about one aspect of his spellcasting. This wasn't the type of thing you wanted to directly touch. It was going to be messy.

My eyes broke away as Alice handed me a pair. Once my fingers were through, the sigil etched there glowed bright becoming a focal point for magic.

Henri's eyes dilated as if he was looking towards the sun, trusting me to keep him from going blind. Their beauty was just a line in between all the green. He truly was a magical thing himself.

If we were meant to be in this position, it should have been doing something holy. Something that created joy. Not resurrecting something dead within someone still full of life.

"I…"

Alice gave her bag a shake. "What do you need?"

My resolve was slipping, and clamped my eyes shut. I couldn't see Henri before me just waiting to be delivered a fate he'd chosen for himself. "I need a card. The Queen."

Alice made a stalling sound. The rustle of things shuffling made it sound like she was digging, but I still couldn't bear to look at the world yet. "Here."

When my eyes opened, a Queen of Hearts was held between us. I frowned as I took it. Studying the profiled face that was mirrored in the opposite direction on the lower half. Oh, how I'd draw this differently if I could.

I flicked the card between my fingers. This was what we'd been dealt. I pressed the card against Henri's forehead and a nervous sheen made it stick there as my hand moved back a few inches from this second focal point. Finishing the other side of a bridge where magic needed to go.

The dead lived within all sorts of things. A body is just the easiest home. Inside the mind of anyone who knew the Queen of Hearts was a piece of her. All I had to do was allow it to blossom.

Henri's balance wavered, muscles going rigid as magic

invaded his mind. Running across paths of memory until it found a now dead thing. There was concerned murmur from the onlookers as his eyes rolled up, head falling back, spine bowing.

Then like a finger snap. His head lulled back, momentum stopping with a hard jolt. "Hello again, Hatter," Henri said, the voice sounding higher than before. "I see you've found your head."

There was no way the Queen ever saw me like this, so she must have access to Henri's knowledge as well as her own. *Gross.*

"I'm not sharing a body either." I watched as Henri stood, then realizes a card is sticking to her forehead and pulls it off. "Guess that makes the score, Me: Two. You: Zip."

Henri laughed. But it's not his laugh. It's a bitter mocking sound. "Always the funny one. I'll admit this body is a bit strange to wear." She inspects the new form as if it is dress that she's uncertain she'll keep. "Guess my nephew has use after all."

Pollux rushed forward, separating us a step further. "Cassandra? We need to know where you died," said the father I absolutely should have been allowed to kill.

"Pol," Cassandra replied fondly, kissing both his cheeks, and unnerving everyone except the possessed among us. Henri's mother seems to whisper his name as if checking for him, but it's far too late for that.

Pollux puts his hands on Henri's shoulder. Both guiding his son back and holding onto his sister at the same time. "Cass, we are fighting for you. But you need to tell us where you were murdered."

"That was not the agreement," Alice reminded. "Don't waste your goodbye time." The reunited siblings ignore her far too easily.

"I don't know," Cassandra starts. Her frown far too big for the Prince's face. "It was in some grass field. Those bloody merry men blindfolded me. Then… it was over so fast."

"If we can't bring you back," Pollux said, hands gripping tighter. "We'll keep you like this."

The Henri/Cass hybrid smiled, while Anna gasped. "Honey! *Our* son!"

"He's still here," Pollux said, turning to me. "Correct?"

I had to push aside thoughts of violence as he dared ask me a fucking thing. Then listen for the melodic notes that mark Henri's consciousness. It's distant, like a memory, but it's there. Somewhere. "Correct."

"You can't keep him!" Alice yelled this time. "Give me my friend back. Now!"

"Grow up, child," Pollux sneered. "Henri has."

I'm not sure what Alice planned on doing, but before she can throw her whole bag at him, Henri's father is forced to deflect a verbal onslaught from his wife.

Pollux gently pulled Anna away to the side to better convince her to let this happen. Citing things like how their family is meant to, destined to, rule.

But fate is just what we call what happens. There's no simple answer. No victory. No justice. Involvement is courting madness.

"Last time, Henri was here to stop me," I said, even whilst looking at Henri's form. "This time, you made sure he isn't."

I didn't need anyone's permission to put an end to this. Taking no one into consideration besides Henri, who glanced towards me, true recognition seemingly lost. "Blood of my blood. Connected through time. With this beginning rhyme. I claim what's mine."

Most mages cast wordlessly. Asking them to explain would be like asking grass to cite how it grows. But when you had the right words everything becomes more powerful. Henri shivered at the sound of my voice and sways as he starts to pass out.

Alice is there first to catch him. They both end up on the ground, but she managed to protect his head from further harm as it rests in her lap. "Is he going to be okay?" she asked, tears darting across her cheeks as she blinks.

I swoop Henri up from her, holding him like I plan on carrying him across the threshold. It's far too easy seeing as his body as no resistance left within it.

"Guards!" Pollux yelled, as his wife continues to scold him with no avail. One rushes out, as a few rush in, surely with more to come.

"Touch any of us," I start, speaking to anyone, everyone, "and I'll rip your lungs out with my bare teeth, just so I never have to hear you give orders again."

"I'd listen," Milo added to my surprise. I glance his way, and he jolts back, stumbling into the seat. Seems doing what he could not has made me a terrifying thing.

Chapter Twenty-Five

"I've ruined something I loved."

We had locked ourselves within a wing of the manor. No one had followed, or made a sound, but I hadn't wanted to risk further annoyance either. Maybe we should have taken him back to his own castle. But I feared jostling Henri further. Adding a location change to possible memory loss wouldn't help a scrambled mind.

"Is that why you didn't answer me before?" Alice asked, venturing to sit on the corner of the bed.

My fingers work their way through Henri's curls as if I could make this all up to him with enough soft gestures.

"Madi, please tell me if he is going to wake up."

Her voice is hurt, and I simply cannot take hurting anyone else I care about today. "He should." I'm happy that's the truth, but there's more of it. "Possession is invasive. I think his consciousness just retreated to protect itself."

I run my hand down the side of his cheek. He's warm.

Chest raising and falling as it should. How did I get from trying to wake a princess to here waiting for him?

"He's not going to care for me after what I did."

"Take it from someone who cares about you," Alice said, "just because you've been alone, doesn't mean you'll always be. I'm here, and you said that's proof things change."

"You are different."

"Seems to me like everything is different. Why not this? You made a bad situation better. That's what he asked, not for you to remove him from the mess entirely."

"I wish he had."

Alice rests her head on my shoulder. "Me too."

We stay with him as he wakes sometime later. The sun is starting to rise, and the room is still awash in candlelight. Alice's stomach is growling, but she refuses to go find food.

Despite being awake again, he doesn't speak much. More physically just going through the motions than interacting with the things around him.

It's the next day before he says anything that isn't expected for manners. Something with real weight to it.

"I don't know which feelings are mine, and what feelings are left over from my aunt." His fingers reach towards his temple and even the slight touch makes him wince.

I rise to go pull the curtains closed on behalf of his headache. "That's how memories work. If you feel something, it becomes yours. But that doesn't mean you have to keep something someone forced on you."

"I very much would like to feel something else right now."

"I can help." My feet return me to where he's seated, and I lower myself to sit on the floor.

"Could you?" His question is so full of hope that my heart breaks further.

Nervously, I lick my lips, then nod. "If you love others. You can love yourself enough to stand up to your family."

"I need help," Henri pleads. "Please, please, help me just see and feel the world like you do. Even for a second."

The floorboards creak as I shift my weight away. "You'd trust me to do magic on you again?" *What an awful idea.*

"I don't blame you, Madison. I pushed you into it. Demanded you do it on my behalf. And you were clearly the one looking out for me after…"

His words trail off, and I'm not sure if he realizes his father wanted to trade his mind in for his aunt's. The expression looks pained as if there's at least some level of awareness of that cruel fact.

"These thoughts," he said with a false start. "How do I really know anything in my head is mine?"

"Here, lace your fingers with mine."

Henri does as instructed. "Now what?"

"Think of something that makes you feel safe."

I expect him to close his eyes, make a wish. But he just keeps looking at me until a smile appears. Only then do his shoulders relax and eyes shut for restful seconds.

"Did you feel anything?"

"Yeah…" He blushed. "I thought you needed potions to

control moods."

"I didn't do anything." My hand pulls back, feeling guilty for touching as if I tricked him. His fingers flex as if wanting to catch me. "It was all you. What others make you feel, what you feel for them. It all starts with you. That's love *you* created."

"Do you think Harts can change?"

My head tilts, trying to hear the letters of the word before deciding it doesn't matter. "Not theirs."

Chapter Twenty-Six

Today had been not a good day. And I didn't have much hope for tomorrow, or the next day either.

Henri's mother had been doting on him all morning. As if she could just fill her every action now with enough love to make up for the absence before. And probably the future evaporation of such open affection.

Anna is the one who convinced Henri to stay here instead of literally returning to an independence of a castle of his own. Things are tense like there's blood in the water that no one wishes to speak about. And Henri only speaks freely when we are alone. But mostly only to try and catch me on some contradiction.

"You said hearts can't change. I'm not only a Prince of Heart in title, but quite literally by blood," he said. The champagne Alice found to celebrate our time all back together is not sitting as well as it usually does. He's argumentative, wanting to debate the past when I just want bubbles.

"You are also the Frog Prince. A title that is yours, and

yours alone. Sure, it may have been molded from their clay, but born from who you truly are. That makes for a new and different work of art entirely."

Alice at least considers this theory. "Poetic," she declared, lifting her glass.

Henri sat back in his seat. "What do you do when faced with a tough problem?"

"Sleep until it's okay."

"What?" Henri chuckled. "Like you take a nap?"

"Not quite, and it's not really sleep either. If there's ever a really big problem that's annoying me I just kind-of stop existing for a while and when I return, it's solved. Or at least less annoying."

"My mother says," Alice interjected, "when one has a problem, they must work hard to find the solution." She looks very thoughtful when speaking, so we wait for her to go on.

"Labor!" She held one finger up. "Labor is the one solution to all of the country's problems." What country she speaks of is still a mystery, but I enjoy it more that way.

"And!" She's louder and more confident since neither of us interrupted her. "Sex work is work!"

"Yeah!" Despite finding her highly educated for her age, I reached over to take the champagne away.

"No one has fun at work." Her tone is just as supportive as before, even though the thought has lost its way.

"Wait," I said, finally giving Alice pause, "I mean, I could have fun with that at least."

Henri choked on his alcohol, covering his mouth. "Sorry, bubbles got me."

Before I can call his bluff, Alice slid her chair out. "I'm

going to change into my nightgown."

Wordlessly we seemed to agree not to speak until she leaves for the other room. "You kill me sometimes," Henri said with a laugh.

"Well, good thing you are in safe hands then."

This was the moment where my night should have ended. He'd smile, and we'd both retire to our beds, feeling safe even at a distance. But as aforementioned time is cruel, and that's not how the story goes.

"I think I should marry someone."

Unless it's to me, that sounded like a stupid idea. Definitely leaning towards what his family would want instead of him. "Is this because I'm a guy?"

"No! I could marry a man if I wanted. They are just meant to have you know…"

I contained my smirk, playing dumb as I watched him get flustered.

"You… the… have non-matching parts that would help make offspring." His face was flush with embarrassment, and I'm probably tickled pink too by his birds and bees summary.

"*Mmm*, matching parts," I said, bring the bottle to my lips.

"Why must you do this to me?" Henri whined, and if he begged for mercy, he'd win far more than he asked for.

"Because you are too cute."

He frowned at my words, a clear sign to be serious.

"You haven't wanted to get married before, what's changed?"

"Everything, Mads."

"That's what I've been saying."

"The Queen is dead."

Wait, no. Well, yes, but irrelevant. "People die all the time." Her death changed nothing. Alice had. We had been.

"Her replacement is missing, presumed dead."

"Oh! He's not dead." I winced, remembering the token of immorality I gave him. Probably still should check in on him though. "Furthest thing from it actually."

Henri's brows lifted over the good news. "Do you think he'll return?"

My stomach soured knowing that he isn't going to. The easy solution out of this mess was changed. By me, ironically, choosing love. "No, I don't think so."

"That's why I should do this. I've messed around plenty."

"Actually, you'll recall you haven't messed around *with* me."

He smirked before continuing on. I didn't wish to flirt or discuss this. I wanted Alice to return.

"You could stay with me. Even though it's time to serve my family. It's not only my duty to them, but to the kingdoms."

I scoffed loudly, and leaned away as far as the chair allowed me. "Neither of those things last forever."

Henri lifted his hands in the air as if to gesture to an audience about how unreasonable I'm being. "And what will last forever?"

"Love."

"What?"

"Love," I repeated. "We can find our own little piece of

Neverland, stay there forever."

"I'm not a child, Mads."

"It's not just for children! You royals just don't understand the things that matter."

"Us royals?" His annoyance is tempered, similar to Queen herself. But far colder and more reserved than she could ever muster. "It's not easy to just run off with you when they are alive. It's not some memory I can ignore. I'm not like—"

The Prince stopped suddenly, knowing his mouth was getting the best of him. If he'd been less comfortable with me, he probably wouldn't have even gotten himself to the point where he was hurtful. Another cruel irony.

"Tell me, Frog Prince, not like *what*."

"I can't give you what you want." Henri's tone is all authority, not showing any wiggle room. Only when he frowned, did I see a hint of him again.

"No," I said, lifting my hat up from the side of the armchair. "You can't give me what *you* want, and that's the real shame in all of this."

"Do you aim to stop me?"

"Yes." I stand there, looking at him casually sitting as he seems willing to throw the rest of his life away. "Yes, I do. Someone needs to save you from your own mistakes."

My mistake was that I'm not used to being nice. I'm used to being an oddity that's feared from an unknowable distance. Befriended occasionally like a wild animal. So, when I let Henri know my intent, he didn't back off. He acted, *quickly*.

"Assumed villain," Henri started. Words just sounding like words until I feel his magic hook into me. My jaw locks, and I can't look away. "As fire fills in. The anger you feel.

181

Becomes all too real. Unsure of where to begin. Within the blooming sin."

It's not the best rhyme, but as I watch Henri walk out of my life, the truth of his spell sinks further in me. Someone comes in, and I don't even care. Can't move. Maybe I'll just this body crumble and start over somewhere else.

"Madi!" Alice called, as she rushed over. I'm planning my great escape as she takes my hat from me. She's digging one moment, pulling out a small vial the next. Then took off the cork and pressed it my mouth, end tilted up.

It's thick and tastes like raw honey. My throat tightens as I piece together that it *is* honey. The magic keeping this body alive senses the danger within the allergic misfire.

Alice helped me sit down as I started coughing up wisps of smoke. My eyes are watering enough to blur my vision as my   stomach spits up the foreign magic and honey unceremoniously up onto the table.

Before I'm even sure I can reply Alice starts speaking. "What happened? I wasn't gone for that long."

"Henri." My throat hurts, and I just ache. Having a body isn't always the best.

"Henri? He did this to you?"

Irritated lungs steal my reply with another coughing fit that produce nothing. So, I just nod and try to settle my body.

"I need to go talk to him." She moves to leave, but I'm able to catch her wrist.

"How did you know what to give me?" Did I tell Alice this body was allergic to things? Even if I had, why would she have thought it wouldn't do more harm? Did they both want to kill me?

"The hat." She took said hat and placed it on my head

as if it would further help. "I just reached out and something furry pushed it into my hand."

"A rabbit?"

"Yeah, probably."

Huh, we did something good that had been returned to us. No one was trying to murder me after all.

"Do you trust me?" Alice followed up with, looking like she was going to run off somewhere.

"...With my life."

"Stay here, I'm going to fix this for the both of you."

I didn't particularly want her to, but I felt like death had brushed his fingers down my throat. And our affair with each other had always been at a distance, so I still needed a moment.

Chapter Twenty-Seven

All that power and even you can't really control death." Pollux looked up from the head of the table towards me like I was a slug that crawled in from the garden. "What a shame. Do have some wine, Alice."

She looked around the table. Notably missing was Henri, and his mother, which left the Duchess who didn't seem thrilled that we had showed up for a meal. I hated that I agreed with her, and really needed to stop taking the back seat in my own life when I didn't enjoy the view.

"I don't see any wine," Alice frowned.

I'm not sure how breakfast with people I hated was meant to fix anything. "Any eggs?" I dared.

"There isn't any," The Duchess replied to us both.

Alice grumbled. "It wasn't very civil to offer it then."

The Duchess poured herself a cup of tea. It smells of lullaby as if she planned to return to bed after this meal. "It wasn't very civil of you to sit down without being invited."

"We were invited?" Alice asked, glancing to me.

All I could do was shrug. I was only here because boredom, which made me willing to bite at their bait. That didn't mean I had any idea what Pollux had been going on about. "What didn't I do with death?"

"Haven't you heard?" Pollux didn't continue on until I turned to properly address him. Probably to annoy me, prove he was worth my full attention.

"Our dear Henri has died." He eyes looked solemn, but he poured himself some water as if dehydration was the greater concern. "My poor son. Losing another Hart so soon is such a waste."

"What? *No*. That can't be... I would have felt that."

Hadn't Alice spoked with him last night? I expected him to be here. I rose from my seat. Maybe leaving and reentering the room would correct this conversation because this was not happening. There'd been no time for him to die.

"What a queer thing you must be," Pollux continued, eyes tracking me across the room. "Do you feel it whenever anything dies?"

"Let's find out." Unsure if my words even sound like words, I advanced on him. Grabbing his collar and yanking him out of his seat. "*Where* is the Frog Prince?"

"Gone," he stammered vaguely until meeting my eyes seem to scare him straight. "I mean his body has been taken to be burned. The carriage just left. It's unclean to let the dead sit around."

"Purity is what you want?" A flare lit within me, engulfing him as its light searched for anything and everything that wasn't strictly his cells. A plentiful bounty, ten to one more than his own. The bacteria in his intestines seemed partially ravenous, and with a little help, multiplied

185

faster to gnaw at him from the inside out. "Fight for it."

He might recover. He might not. Either way there'd be no sitting out a war raging within his own body. I didn't care to find out the winner and walked through the manor looking for what I wanted.

The estate was large, but my field of view can grow infinitely. My arms were out at my sides, magic reached out even further. Touched anything once living in this house. The deer head over a dusty mantel. Trees made into flooring bearing the weight of everything. Formally dead bugs flipped over from their backs and began to search along with me.

Henri wasn't in this wing. I turned down another hall. Sense growing as wide was my frustrations. Because I hadn't found a single remain of him anywhere on this cursed ground.

The voices of the dead howled in a deafening chorus as my awareness grew more divine. When I yelled, demanding to know where Henri was, the bones of naturally buried animals and skeletons in man-made graves rose.

Each risen form flickering a new viewpoint into the growing patchwork of sights, sounds, smells. All that was once alive responded to my force of will. Collections of bones pulled themselves up on decaying limbs, threaded back together by a golden wirework of magic. The whole house of macabre trophies turned into a looking glass.

Time was always cruel to lovers. No matter how much it gave you, it was never enough. I'd make him pay. Every royal heart would pay for taking what had been mine.

"You always were a little royal chaser," a nasty voice in my head said. All these years and I never learned how to fully exorcise comments made forever ago. "Gold digger."

Why was the world so loud with random thoughts?

Those things weren't true. Had never been true. All I wanted was to run the shop. And have the type of love people wrote fondly about. Oh, how tales were often told by those who wanted to be the worshipped hero. They never included strange things like me.

All monarchs are bastards. I saved Malcolm from that fate, and I could certainly save myself from it too. I couldn't save Henri. I couldn't save Henri. I couldn't. I couldn't. I couldn't.

My scream drowned out the thought. More thunder than human. The clouds cracked and poured out everything they had to offer. Raindrops adding further chorus for growth as sprigs of green pushed up from between rocks. Life and death were mine, how dare anyone keep them from me.

I must find his body. I could reach anything in life or death. Where was he? He must exist somewhere.

"Madi!" Alice yelled from afar. She was coming towards me, tracked by all the other undead things as I stepped onto the road wondering if Pollux wasn't lying about taking the body elsewhere for burning.

"Not now, Alice."

Magic crept over a fossil in a far-off library. The creature's pieces had been incorrectly placed together to make something that never had been. A false history of what had once existed.

The creature broke free, fallen from the frozen flight it was forced into over the bookshelves. Snapping into place as it hits the ground, and now moved, as nature intended.

Without lying a finger on anything, I knew there's nothing within the walls or gardens that remained untouched by me.

"Madi!" Alice yelled again as she neared me. She stamped a foot, and the vibration catches my attention deeper than her words. "It's poor manners to ignore your friends."

"Manners are the least of my worries, dear."

Alice less came into view, then shifted into the center of it. I bent down, hand to dirt, and reached out for anyone down this road to answer my call. "My patience is stretched so very thin. If you have something to say, out with it."

"That's what I've trying to tell you! We had a plan."

We? What plan? There was no plan.

Without a conscious thought of my own, a rotting hand finds Pollux's ankle, and teeth bite into his leg before the skeleton is even fully standing. Even unable to raise to its full height seemed pleased in eating the rich as dessert best served cold.

Alice dared to touch me. Taking my arm, pulling me further away from those who are fleeing and all the beautiful helpful dead things. And I let her since this specific body isn't all the important in the grand scope of things.

Their connections in my head dissolve suddenly as I'm brought to a meadow with an uncovered carriage that sits without any horse to pull it. No horses had ever even died nearby.

Alice jumps up on the large wheel and pulls back a sheet to reveal Henri lying peacefully. Breath halted in his chest, but not dead either.

"We devised a plan to get him out of there," Alice started to explain, looking back towards me. "We didn't mean for you to get so upset. I was going to tell you once we were alone, but I didn't account that vile Hart taunting you again."

I blinked back my surprise, feeling quite small within only one body again. Alice removed a black rose that had been placed between his folded hands. The hasty movement pricked blood, spilling a drop onto a thorn. As it flows, he inhales sharply.

Henri further stirred, and I watch in silence as if I've never seen a body move before. He gave a soft smile to Alice as she hops off the wheel. "Hi Madison, miss *mm*—"

His words are cut off as I strode over. Cradling the back of his head in my hands as I smash our mouths together. The surprise melts away into a tender warmth. The unmistakable feeling of life.

I sighed in relief, pulling away just enough to rest my forehead on his. "I was going crazy trying to find you. I didn't understand why I couldn't."

"You say you're crazy about me?" Henri teased, before reaching up to touch my cheek. "Sorry I made a pit stop between life and death. And... for everything else. You made me realize my family would never accept me. That my only freedom from them might be in death. So, I faked it."

"I did *not* say anything like that!"

Alice hopped into the front of the wagon. Even though I don't know how she planned to drive it anywhere right now. "I thought everyone was going to catch on. But lullaby tea is no joke, and you accidentally sold it hard by thinking the hastiness was them keeping you two apart. I think that's what really cinched it."

"A family full of nothing but fear of things looking a strange is quick to judge and cast out," Henri added.

"I did at imply that." Heat rose to my cheeks, and a bone deep relief sets in, making me just want to fall the ground and laugh at the absurdity of this situation.

Instead, I step out of reach of anyone and cleared my throat. More embarrassed than anything else after the fact. "I mean... yeah, I wasn't that worried or anything."

Alice turned to Henri. "There were *soo* many dead bodies at your parent's place. Some where all gross and sticky."

Henri tried to smile, but mostly scrounges up his nose probably trying not to picture it in too much detail. It's so adorable I could to die. Why did he have to be so damn fine all the time?

Whatever God existed I was going to kiss them for making this person so perfect. Every creation before him was just practice.

"What are you scheming over there?" Henri asked, as he climbs out of the wagon.

"Hmm? I wasn't thinking anything." I crossed my arms over my chest with the maturity of an immortal thing. "Just trying to figure out how to get us moving given the lack of four-legged assistance."

"We have to walk," Alice said, "I bribed the original driver to bring Henri here in exchange for him taking the horse for himself. The Hart's love their animals more than their staff so it was probably a jackpot."

"Selectively bred," Henri bitterly added, "like all things they care about."

His following frown makes me want to punch the sun. So, I try to find something reasonable. "The cellist?"

Henri nodded. "The only other even mildly trustworthy person back there. Where should we go now?"

This plan wasn't very prepared. "You're asking me?"

"Of course," Henri started off, offering Alice a hand down before his attention came back to rest with me. "If anyone knows how to put the 'fun' in 'funeral' it would be you."

Alice agrees as if this is the truest statement that could be, and I can't help but smile at the friends I've gathered.

Part Three: All Sales Are Future
Chapter Twenty-Eight

The world is capable of providing for everyone's needs, so I glanced around the area surrounding us.

This spot of land hasn't even so much as a vegetable patch. Near things, like the road and a lake, but hadn't been valued for much besides being out of the way. The patchwork of mixed grass, clover, and a single rabbit sit silently as the wind came through as if also waiting for my decision.

Wait, a rabbit. I slowly walked over to the creature, worried if I moved too quick it would bolt off. The rabbit's small eyes lifted up to me. "Please thank your kind for helping us. Might you also have a suggestion of where to go next?"

The nose wiggle said it all. Well, said that the rabbit knew it was being spoken to at least. His back legs thumped on the ground. A hole opened where he touched. The burrow started as nothing wider than what the rabbit needed, but as it leaped in the tunnel opened up large enough for a person.

I glanced back towards my friends with a smile before dropping in. The usual graceful fall was replaced with a fast descent, and I wasn't given a moment to stop and choose a direction as pinhole of light appeared. Flung through, I landed on my back hard against the ground on the other side.

A few seconds later, Alice found herself spat out, coming to a rolling stop a few feet away with a laugh. While watching her, I had failed it look up at what else was coming next. And Henri dropped on top of me.

"Sorry." Henri was quick to push himself up with his arms, and invertedly pressed his crotch further into mine. "Again."

Fuck'n rabbits, I thought with a smirk, they'd planned for that. I played suggestively innocent. "For what? Using my body to break your fall?"

If he were any closer, he'd been able to feel my words against his lips instead of just hearing them. "That's one way to put it."

"Do you wish to find another?"

His intense gaze dipped to my mouth for a moment. "No, because I'm not sorry," he corrected himself. "Rather thankful actually."

"Guys?" Alice asked, as we both glanced towards her. She was looking around not recognizing her surroundings. "Where are we?"

"This is my castle, and my room." Henri pulled back the rest of the way and stood. "Although, I'm not sure why we are here."

My theory was weak since it would have involved the bed, and I don't believe wild animals even shared the concept.

"What would you do?" Henri asked, turning back to me. The tone quite different than before, body language more tense.

"I'm an abolitionist, love."

The Prince smiled at me, and I believed in fairy tale romances.

"Okay, let me figure this out." Henri paced around his room, found a bag, and asked Alice to hold it open for him. He gathered a few things, clothes mostly, and dropped them into the very unmagically sized space.

"What else do I have?" he mumbled to himself, before looking up to Alice in front of him. "My mirrors. Alice, would you like to see your home?"

Alice's eyes went wide. "Can I go home?"

"We can try, just need to show us where it is first," Henri said. "Will you watch my stuff? I'll go get them ready."

Her hands tightened on the straps. "I'll be the best bagman ever."

When Henri left the room, I followed as if he was a stage play I had been watching. This seemed to surprise, but not offend, Alice as she joined us.

We were brought down a long windowless hall. I couldn't see anything in the low light but could feel the layers of magic soaked into the stone walls.

As Henri started to light candles the room's purpose became clear as the hall of mirrors slowly illumined. Towards the back was an altar, framed beautifully by the gold trimmed collection.

"Once the smoke builds, we'll be able to ask them where your home is," Henri said, "and hopefully how to get you there."

"Alright." Alice beamed for a bright second. "Thank you."

"Do you want to go home?" I asked.

"I like it here, but..." She skewed her lips over to the side. "Might be getting that time. I'd like to know if travel between is possible. I sometimes fear I'll suddenly wake up back home and never see anyone I met here again."

I reached for her hand, giving it a squeeze. "We're real. If there is anything I know for certain, it's that. And anything that's real can be found again."

As we waited, there were two other curious things found within the Frog Prince's castle. The first was that the literal music had left. The cellist had returned here before us and left a note that the band joined him to find their next gig.

He rode the whole way, so we must have lost some time since he had beaten us here. Nothing was covered in a thick layer of dust so it couldn't have been too long.

The second involved even more candles. This time they were arranged around the castle's private hot spring. A small damp rocky area on the lowest level that suggested the castle was built around this naturally made gift. The candles were set along the edge, sitting safely within clear glass and on small river rocks.

"Did you light these as well to... set the mood?" The idea that this had been done for me was a delight.

Henri nodded, movement jerky as if he were uncertain of what to do, where to be, or how to stand. "Yes, I uh, wanted tonight to be magical."

I watched as the smoke twisted up serving no magical purpose besides tinting the air with a light flowery scent. "Is that so?"

"Turn of phrase," Henri said softly. He took a step closer, seeming to gain reassurance as he laced his fingers in mine. "In truth, I don't know how to woo someone. And Alice and I still felt guilty after... before. She's the one that mentioned to me that candles have other purposes where she comes from."

I would have pulled him closer, kissed him silent, if I didn't enjoy the sound of his voice so much. The admission that I could be hurt or need care mattered. "This is a respectable showing."

"Thanks," Henri said, smile flickering like the wicks. "So, do you forgive me?"

"That depends."

His expression dimmed, frowning deepening as my hand slipped free. "On what?"

I ventured a toe into the water to test its temperature. "If you're going to be continue to be you."

He didn't speak for a long moment, and I considered submerging myself in the hot spring's warmth without waiting any further for a reply.

"You make me feel..." Henri started, clearly struggling as I turn to look over my shoulder at him. "Like freedom is a real thing. That I can be myself. Or at least figure out who that is."

"I do," I said, bit out of time. "Forgive you, that is."

Henri pushed his curls back behind his ears, looking filled to the brim with a young hopefulness.

"You could also skinny dip," I teased. "Wouldn't hurt with making things up to me."

Henri moved closer; eyes locked on me. His hands shifted forward as if to undo his belt.

Then dipped lower into the water. As a splash came my way, he pulled on an expression that is meant to look perfectly innocent. "Me in the nude? You're the one with wet clothes."

I shake the pant leg which took most of it. "Truly, you must save yourself from this horrid fate."

"I don't know about that." He pressed his lips together in mock consideration before smirking. "You look good wet."

"The Frog Prince would look better." I stand my ground, which happens to be more of a puddled entrance to the hot spring. But still. "It's in your blood."

"Perhaps." That's all he said. One single word, and he's off staring at me like I'm a thing not meant to be touched.

"Join me."

"I… can't right now." He took a step back, to my further confusion. "There's something important I just remembered I have to do."

At those words, he seemed to slip into his past self. I sigh and dip into the water, clothes, and all. The hot spring's silky warmth slides in between everything promising comfort all the same.

"Madison," Henri said, and I'm mildly surprised he is even still here. "Just wait for me a little moment longer."

Alice squeaked as she entered. Her hands flying to cover her eyes.

Given that I had shed some clothes after they had gotten progressively waterlogged it wasn't all that unreasonable. My shirt was in dripping pile along the edge.

"Are you decent?"

"Not normally, but I'm still largely dressed."

"Can you please explain why Henri feverishly stormed into his study? What did you say?"

"Hey now, I have feelings too."

Alice frowned. "I'm sorry, I didn't mean to blame you. I just don't know why you aren't together."

"That makes the two of us." I pushed myself out of the pool. "Show me?"

My wet footprints mark the path to the study. And there I found my love standing behind a desk, as if sitting would limit his ability to read the four books he was flipping through at once. "You left me to go read?"

"I just realized," he began to say, losing the thought as he glanced at the wood floors before refocusing on the nearest book. "Here, look. It's the solution Prince Phillip has been looking for."

Hadn't the slightest idea of what he was going on about, so I stepped closer. Trying my best not to drip as I leaned over the papers on the desk. "A family tree?"

"Yours."

By the stars, he's lost it. We'll be forever mad together now. "You're mistaken. That's Aurora's."

"Madison Hatterson." He pushed the book closer,

tapping near the roots. "Aurora is your great great grandniece."

"Madi doesn't look that old."

"Not in this body, no. His original," Henri explained, "Aurora's grandmother wasn't a royal. She married a prince. Thus, gaining her a title. Whenever this happens the royals dig up records and preserve the information so they can pretend that all royals were born noteworthy."

Henri walked around to the front of the desk. Turning back only for a second to grab a different book to read from. "The blood of an agreement is thicker than the water of the womb." His eyes lifted from the text. "It's how you brought me back from my aunt's control. And it's how you can reach the Princess."

"Okay, but he doesn't have that body anymore." Alice turned from the books to glance over to me. "Is just the magic keeping you here enough?"

I consider this and attempted to come to some universal truth about the connections between people. "All lost things can be found."

Chapter Twenty-Nine

I had the habit of living out of order. And today's ritual of returning someone who became very dear to me home did not feel like an exception to that. Was it really time to say goodbye?

"Wake," commanded Henri, and the magic brewing against mirror's glass surface listened and stirred the images within.

Alice stood in the middle of it all, surrounded by a ring of salt that I made sure not to cross. They both seemed fine when walking over it, but I never trusted anything that claimed to protect. One person's 'protection' could mean another's destruction.

"Oh!" Alice exclaimed as the mirrors refection's dimmed into a dark cool void. "It tickles."

"Show me home," Henri instructed, sounding awfully close to Alice's original request of me. A large clock face appeared first, then the mirrors motionlessly seemed to tilt to show the building it was on.

Just as the image reached the ground a fog rolled in obscuring the image. Alice didn't seem any worse for it as she silently watched.

The shadows in the side mirrors seemed to take shape, but still removed from any color. Images shifted to show a fireplace, glass jars, then a headless mannequin standing by the front door.

A giggle bubbled out of me.

"This isn't somewhere I know," Henri said, turning to me. "Do you?"

I nodded; attention affixed to Alice. "Do you know how to get home, dear?"

"Claudia," Alice said, breathing the name out like a prayer. Hands coming to her mouth as to catch the sound. "My heart is with her."

"Mads?" Henri prompted, looking for me to explain.

"Claudia's my..." How does one explain the fondness I had for her? This idea of my timeless friend finding kinship within a stranger not of our world. How Claudia was the only person or thing in any of the lands that I knew would outlive me. Yet still would carry a memory of whatever I left. "Claudia's my heir."

"End this," Henri said, smiling softy and the magic settled back into translucent hanging smoke. He took Alice's hand, guiding her carefully over the salt line since the revelation she received seemed to have stunned her.

She was brought over to sit along the edge of the raised platform. Henri whispered something, and she shook her head. "I'm fine, I just need a moment."

When he stood back up, he breathed in deeply. The smokey magic flexed along with him. "You know, for all this magic. All these mirrors. All my searching..." His eyes found mine as I continued to near silently watched the show. "I never saw *you*."

"Maybe you didn't, not like this at least."

"What do you mean?"

"I woke up in this body shortly before finding Alice. If you had seen me, it wouldn't have been…" My hand gestured towards the rest of my body. "Me."

Henri crossed the distance between us in two strides. Pulling my face closer as if knowing his fingers could reach me first. Before his mouth captured mine and brought me greedily further against him.

When his tongue slipped into my mouth, I couldn't have felt a bigger part of the scene. Elevated from random audience member to chosen by the leading man for the world to see.

An amused confusion followed the enjoyment when we stopped kissing. "Was I right?"

"I have no idea," he confessed. "I just love how your mind works. I love you."

"I love you. You're mad."

He nuzzled his nose against mine, catching another kiss. "Absolutely crazy about you."

I ran a hand across the back of a throne that had no royal to occupy it. What would this castle turn into once abandoned?

"Are you ready?" Henri asked. He had walked in like a page boy wearing a crown from a new world order that wasn't here yet. "Alice is checking for any horses, and I gathered the remaining food for our trips. If we have to walk, maybe the gold will get us some helpful attention."

I nodded at the crown, and walked around the throne, taking a seat while reliving some far-off memory.

"What are you doing?" Henri asked, near laugh.

"Just thinking how I got here."

"You know…" He licked his lips before continuing. "We won't be coming this way again. Maybe you should have that reward now. You'll be owed one soon."

I pushed myself back to sit flush against the throne's unforgiving back, feeling all the more proper for it. "Being owed is not how love works."

He smiled. "Okay, a promise then."

"Here?"

He nodded. "Here and now."

Well, alright.

How exactly I got to this day, or in the literal seat of power, with Henri on his knees before me undoing my pants with a sense of reverence, no longer mattered to me.

What soon mattered much more was the feeling underneath my fingers as they gripped both hair and crown to hold on for dear life as Henri took my cock so deep in his mouth it drove me wild with every move.

My moans of pleasure echoed back to me in harmony within the throne room's wonderous acoustics. I felt limitless like my consciousness filled entire place. Driven by the desire a body was able to feel more than any tangible thought. Lack of experience meant nothing when it came to someone you cared about making it their mission to take everything you had to offer.

Henri might have been a virgin, but everyone who hadn't been willing to wait for him was missing out. There was something primal and shared between us as we chased a peak of the enjoyment that could be felt this way. Animalistically beyond words, yet still in communion.

I came hard with a gasp that didn't quite suck in air. Henri wiped his mouth on my inner thigh causing another small quake within me.

"I got you," Henri said, placing a hand on mine where they had been grasping the arm rests. My body found myself thankful he hadn't pressed on. So overstimulated that I might have otherwise fallen out of this one and skipped the next two entirely. "Remember to breathe."

Almost forgot living things needed to do that. Inhale. Exhale. My body relaxed into the seat, able to better appreciate the afterglow.

Only then did Henri stand, making me realize he'd actively been trying not to crowd me. I loved one considerate man.

If necromancy was my connection to everything, being with Henri was far more personal. On this literally intimate front, and all others that I cared about.

"I didn't make a mess," he said with a sense of pride to himself and looking almost as flushed as I felt. "Ready to go save the day?"

Inhale. Exhale. I stood up, surprised at the loyalty my knees showed in not buckling, and I fastened my belts. "Lead the way."

Chapter Thirty

To been honest, I thought nothing of the plight of Prince Phillip's kingdom until the road brought us to an endless long stretch of dead thorn bushes.

"What happened here?" Alice scoped up a drooping rose bud in her hands. "These plants were doing fine the last time we were here. Did we do something?"

"Killing is the literal opposite of my nature."

Alice pulled her hands back, and the rose did look worse after she had touched it.

"The things you rise can kill people," Henri countered, seemingly amused by my statement. "You do know that, right?"

"Living things kill other living things all the time. It is the nature of the world. Hardly see how I'm to blame." My answer started as a defense, but there was a useful truth within them.

My hand hovered over the withered rose, reaching

around the death, and lifting it out. Life snagged against the whole of the briar, knotted somewhere deeper within. "Princess Aurora is dying. The soil is running out of magic to keep her alive. This is all still Prince Phillip's doing."

Henri pressed his lips into a thin line, thinking for a moment before declaring we needed to make a run for it. I suddenly wished the quartet had left us with a single horse as we flat outran towards the castle.

Alice collapsed at the gates upon the feet of one of Prince Phillip's guards.

Henri slowed just enough to pull up an air of authority and decorum. "I must see Phillip," he declared, before grabbing my hand and pulling me forward.

The guard looked to follow after the first wave of confusion washed over him, but Alice tugged on his pant leg. "Water? Please, sir."

The bewildered rumbling continued as Henri walked down the halls. Clearly knowing where he was going, despite every onlooker's expression that suggested we were in the wrong place.

We found Prince Phillip leaning over Aurora with his head pressed into her chest. Shoulders trembling as if he was crying.

Phillip glanced up at the commotion that rolled in, eyes bloodshot as he looked over the fellow prince. "Henri?" he asked kindly, then his eyes narrowed. "*Hatter.*"

If we had the time, I would have reminded Phillip that he had been the one to threaten me.

"Don't be an ass, Phillip. We are here to help." Henri turned to look at me, giving my hand an encouraging squeeze before letting go.

I moved up the small rising steps needed to reach

Aurora, as Henri continued to speak to the heartbroken Prince. "We found the spell needed to wake her."

"What?" Phillip breathed the words so softly, even leaning away as I moved to sit next to Aurora that I wondered if he was in shock.

The first time I had seen what he had done here, I thought it was a spell that simply kept her frozen in time. One that had grown messy, because hope was always messy. Even now as love literally wept over a body as the world outside died, there was still faith in Phillip that believed a miracle would arrive. *Magic* that had now returned in the form of her great great grand ancestor.

"What are you doing?" Phillip asked.

"Hush," Henri said on behalf of my focus.

I picked the rose up between her hands, finding it as beautiful as the one I gave the Beast. A similar one had been in Henri's hands when I thought he'd been lost. This was the single remaining rose blooming in Phillip's whole kingdom.

This close to her death without the symphony of magic coming in from everywhere I could hear the notes that made up Aurora.

I pressed my hand into the flower's stem as tight as I could. Thorns broke my skin, reaching deep enough to touch the magic within. As the blood dropped from the flower onto the dress below, the weight of the world rested above us.

"Blood of my blood," I enchanted, hoping it's not too dissimilar within this body. One that easily would have been forgotten if it hadn't fallen in love with a prince. *Everyone is connected to each other.*

My hand bleeds freely listening to the hum of the magic. "Connected through time. With this beginning rhyme, I claim what's mine."

Calling to Henri had been easy. Our chosen bond was much more powerful than the water of a distantly familiar kin. My hand bled unnaturally, running slickly down my wrist. It could have filled a cup as dizziness started to threaten my concentration.

The added weight of my spell fractured like glass, cutting the connection between Aurora and defensive briar wall. Magic struck against what should be dead and sparked life once more. Effortlessly, the sleeping princess opened her eyes as her heart began to beat again.

It needed more effort than it should, but I forced my fingers to open. Dropping the rose onto the chest of a woman who starts sitting up from her strange nightmare.

Or maybe that's mine too. My hand is covered in blood that I'm already convinced will never stop hurting as she recovers her bearings.

"Madi!" Alice yelled, rushing up to my side. "You did it. You don't have to bleed for anyone else anymore."

Just like pleasure, pain isn't summoned with a completely willful thought of my own. It's just what my body tells me is happening. And shit, it's right again, this is agony.

Wordlessly, Henri takes my hand in both of his as if to put pressure on the tiny cuts. His touch burns, causing a whine, too out of my mind to understand why.

"Aurora, I can't believe you're back," Phillip said, finding new tears within him.

"What happened? What's going on, my love?" she asked, unaware of the trauma her unwilful absence caused. My magic feels *there*, not with the body I'm meant to inhabit.

"I'm not letting go either." The voice is misplaced, and

with a few slow blinks, Henri comes into focus and is indeed still holding my hand. "Stay with me."

I... *I want to*. "Is it bad?"

Henri carefully moved his hand back to look at the pricks that should never be a mortal wound. "I stopped the bleeding. With rest you should be able to heal further yourself."

"Yeah." I agreed without even looking at my hand. The gravity of the situation was *him*. It had been this whole time. A bright guiding light that Alice kept reflecting the love of when he was gone from my sight. Only after this realization did I venture to actually inspect my hand. There's small blisters where I had been hurt. That's why his touch was too hot.

Henri turned to Prince Phillip, and the now awake Princess Aurora. They too seemed like a happy little celestial system of their own. "Do me a favor," Henri asked.

"Anything," Phillip answered.

"Leave us out of how Aurora woke up."

This seemed to confuse her further. "You don't want the credit for saving me?"

"A life for a life. If you hear that I'm dead, pretend that it's true."

"What? Where are you going?" Aurora asked, then glanced to Phillip as if he had the answers.

"We have somewhere else to go," Henri said, looking to Alice next to us. "Isn't that, right?"

Alice threw her hands around me as if I was suddenly safe enough to be touched again. "I was so scared! You're too important for me to just run off to someone else. I'm never ever ever going to ask for you to solve other people's problems again."

Aww, I'm so loved.

Chapter Thirty-One

Claudia was out of sorts when we made it back to the shop. So, I had Alice and Henri wait with the Caterpillar, who grew a happy degree fatter since the last time we'd seen him.

"It's okay if you love someone back," I said, being direct since Claudia was literally crushing her feelings between pestle and mortar at the moment. "It's not against the rules."

"You don't get to talk to me about failing for anyone when you brought back fucking royalty." She doesn't even glance my way, focused on rolling the crushed sticky feelings between her palms. Placed back down on the table, they sat looking like pulled taffy.

"Let me help." I grabbed a palette knife and offered to divide up what she was working on into bite-size pieces. She eyed me warily and goes back to working out her feelings with the mortar.

"He isn't fucking me actually." The subject is just off

topic from what she is avoiding that I hope I'm able to get her to open up. Rather than turning the shop into a full-time pharmacy for candied feelings.

"That makes it worse, because that means you actually care to keep them around."

"I can date Henri," I said, carefully side stepping the tangent, "because I know he's probably going to die before me. And yet, I'm still able to enjoy his presence."

Her pestle comes down particularly hard, but I push on.

"You're lamenting that there won't ever be enough time with Alice to the point you'd forgo whatever time is offered."

"You don't know how I feel." The words are pure defense, and a quite futile one since she'd been bottling them up within sight.

"You're letting time get the best of you."

Claudia's shoulders slump as she actually felt the heaviness of her own feelings. "He is quite cruel."

I smiled, thinking she's doing better with things than giving herself credit for. "Love makes plenty mad. You don't need to figure everything out while I'm still around anyway." As I pulled her into a hug, she rests her head against me.

"You deserve whatever you want." My words are a whisper into her hair, and I kiss her head. "Live in the moment, Claudia. Not a past one, and not one that hasn't happened yet."

"Can she stay in the shop with me? Is that allowed?"

I guide her back, hands on her shoulders. "Who owns this shop?"

"I do."

"Then that's who makes the rules you live by."

Claudia decided her rules include cleaning before she has guests over. So, I lent a hand before we head out of the shop to meet up with friends.

Henri and Alice are where I left them, sitting at the same table. The main difference is they've attracted a small fluffle of rabbits. A few lay stretched out at Alice's feet, while one is sitting quite proper in her lap. There's a few more sat on the ground around them.

It's clear they trust Alice most, since Henri has an outstretched arm holding out a basil leaf from his salad. The rabbit remains just out of reach wiggling their noise.

"I'm sorry, Miss Alice." Claudia curtseys and the most of the rabbits scatter, leaving only one in Alice's lap. Likely unwilling to give up the pets.

"Your Highness," Claudia said, awkwardly a few seconds after to Henri. "I'm not used to so many visitors at once."

"Please call me Henri." He stands to bow before offering Claudia his seat.

Claudia's even more careful around nobility than the rabbits. So, I give her a gentle push and she takes the chair across from Alice. *There, perfect.* Henri and I are together, and the girls are too.

"Please, don't worry," Alice said, as she scooped the rabbit up in her hands. "I made some friends while waiting."

"They are good neighbors," Claudia said, offering her finger out for the rabbit to sniff.

Henri turned to me. "Where are we staying?"

"Oh, I don't know." I suspect Alice will stay in the shop with Claudia, but four people would be a bit tight. "I don't live here."

"Is there an inn?"

I shake my head. "The rabbits might let us stay with them. Everything would be probably quite small for us though. The Caterpillar might have some mushroom—"

He chuckles, thinking I'm joking. "I wonder if there's any more favors I could ask." Henri takes two steps towards the shops before snapping his fingers, spinning back around. "Jasmine!"

"Another Princess of Heart? How does that help?"

"Her kingdom is far enough away that none of my family ever goes there. We can make an exchange for asylum."

"You can do that?"

He stepped back, lifting my chin up with the tips of his fingers. "We can do anything we want."

I grinned, never expecting insurrection to be so tender.

Chapter Thirty-Two

Not to give the Hart's an ounce of credit, but I saw why they did not travel this way often. First of all, it was expensive. I didn't know the way, so we had to trade Henri's solid gold crown for two camels who had memories of their home.

Second, it was hot. The sun refused to yield out here, and our only reprise was layers of clothes to keep it directly off our skin. At night, our camels liked to sleep so we sat close to each other and them for the added warmth.

"I can't believe you got me to leave my castle for…" Henri started to gesture to a sea of nothing but sand and was interrupted by a fly buzzing by his face.

"Yeah, sorry about that," I said. This place wasn't great. Dry as anywhere I could imagine. All the food we'd brought spoiled in the heat. I rolled an orange that became far too soft around in my hands trying to put some life back into it.

My fingers dug in, and juice spritzed out. Smiling softly to myself I peeled it further, carefully taking white strings off that remained. "Here."

Henri blinked down at the fruit, staring at it even after he took it from me. "Thank you."

"I know it's not a chocolate covered strawberry or anything."

He quickly shook his head. "Oranges are actually my favorite."

"I can't wait to learn absolutely everything about you."

He leaned in to kiss me, and a slight blush warmed up my life further.

As I sat back, he slipped an orange slice between my lips. "How much longer do you wager?"

"Couple days, at least."

"Okay, you'll need another then." Henri separated another slice before feeding it to me.

The juice was as sweet as him, nourishing in a way that had nothing to do with the actual orange itself. "Do you always plan on us taking care of each other?"

"I do."

The honor of watching over us next was mine as he fell asleep late in the night. In the early morning, our camels decided it was time to start moving again.

Seeing Jasmine's kingdom felt like a mirage. Spires marked the tallest points within the city. A place that sat on top of an equally angular cliffside. I couldn't see water but wouldn't have trusted any of my senses if I had.

We arrived as the sun set, making the sky a beautiful mixture of pink, purple, and blue. Those colors were the only thing I trusted at the moment.

"Henri, what will we do if Jasmine doesn't want to have us here?"

"I'll sleep in the streets with you if we must." His eyes caught mine and held a seriousness that had a depth of its own. "I'm not going back."

All we had left to trade was paper. The legal deeds to Henri's lands should have great value, but things only had worth if multiple parties agreed. Technically, the 'dead' couldn't make trades, so I wasn't sure how he was going to play this.

Henri would have to play royal again to claim anything. Nearly every part of this plan was at the will of the those in power here. Even the most generous ruler gave arbitrary, and what is corruption if not arbitration that someone else had paid for?

"Madison," Henri said, pulling me out of my thoughts. By the concerned look on his face, he knew that truth too. "I don't know exactly what you are thinking. But I got this. I was raised to deal with rulers."

That's exactly what worried me.

The wind brought in clean air, scented by the tang of limestone and dust. Tall rock formations yielded to the buildings here replacing the natural skyline with an equally jagged horizon.

There were enough people within the city walls that our presence went unnoticed. If this place had a tourist bureau, I'd at least know who to ask for directions.

"I must confess I have no idea where to go," Henri said, coming to stop at the corner of a building that wasn't getting much foot traffic.

"To find royalty one normally looks for the biggest tallest building in the area." Everything here looked roughly equal to each other. Some were taller, but others were wider. Maybe the castle was set back away from the city itself.

"Could you…" Henri started, seeming unsure how he wanted to phrase his desire, "make a commotion? Then the powers that be will find us."

Stars, what a loveable thing he was. I could definitely do as he asked.

Under the sun-faded fabric of the bazaar, my focus reached past the shopkeepers, and the crowd's footsteps. Below the meats cooking over fire. To just under the surface where a world full of crawling things. And among them, their dead.

Attention singularly on scorpions, the arachnid worked their way up to the surface. Pushing through the sand with whatever they had died without. Some missing stringers, or heads, while others moved with limited limbs.

While we hadn't been noticed before, that changed as the creatures made a ring around us. The commotion rippled through the crowd clearing it and carrying along the message that something of note was here.

Soon soldiers flowed in to replace the influx of people retreating. They pointed their weapons toward us but didn't advance. The scorpions thought of them no different than any other person.

One of the soldiers broke the unspoken barrier, taking a step closer. He showed no fear as a scorpion crawled up and over his foot. His heavy cloth armor had a tree over the thick trunk of his chest. Any point of his body, from arms to waist to a leg were equally as dense as the symbol itself.

Despite the leadership, he stood as if he was never comfortable. Hands near his hips, making his stance even wider as if his muscles wouldn't allow his arms to even rest casually along his side. "Cease this nonsense now," he ordered.

I only followed Henri's requests, so I glanced over to him. Henri nodded, and my let my control of the creatures slip. The ones fairest from me ran out of magic first as their collective motion came to waved rest nearest to us.

"As a Prince of Heart," Henri said authoritatively. "I request an audience with Princess Jasmine at once."

The solider looked over Henri like he could use him as a toothpick instead of following his rule. "Do you have something to prove you are who you say?"

Henri stood up straighter in surprise. Recognition of him clearly did not go out this far. "Yes, of course." He stepped forward, moving his bag in front of him.

The solider watched as Henri pulled out some sort of identification that had gold leaf along one side. He grunted at the papers. "And the bugs?"

Rude. Scorpions have eight legs. Well, most of them still did.

"It is a matter of outmost haste," Henri said, and reminded me why he did all the talking. "The safety of the kingdoms is at risk."

"Autar," the man said, half turning his head towards another man in the guard. "Inform Princess Jasmine."

A bear of a man in his own right stepped forward. Their trimmed beards matched, but this man kept his hair cut shorter to match the other soldiers. "Certainly, Hadi." He bowed, then was off.

Hadi nodded over towards me. "And he is?"

"The Mad Hatter," I said, taking a step forward.

"Clearly."

I tilted my head, not following. If he hadn't known Henri, there was even less of a chance for me to be known.

My confusion seemed to translate as Hadi's lip curled up in disgust. "Only someone mad would bring those things back."

"Ah, truly." I smiled, making my mind up that I liked this guard captain.

We waited until Autar returned with a woman who caused everyone's movements to ripple like her presence was the ocean. Her outfit was layered in a flowy teal. The movement all suggested magic, and the reverence of those around her made up for the lack of it.

Her chin was held high, long black ponytail decisively whipping, as her eyes searched for Henri. "Is it the Wolf King? Have you found him?"

"He's not returning, Jasmine," Henri started, giving the news a beat. "But I have an offer for you."

"I'm not traveling for another election."

"That's not my offer." Henri smiled slightly. "I want to give you my titles."

"What? Why? What's going on?"

"I want out," Henri said sharply. "In exchange for my kingdom, we want to live here under your protection."

She paused to fill in what wasn't being said, as much as what was. "Protection from the Harts? Won't they fight me for it?"

At the end of the day, Henri only meant one thing to his family. Someone capable of holding the land in their name. A pawn that had been better suited for outside approval. They never suspected Henri could just opt out.

Agency looked damn fine on him.

"Sure," Henri conceded to Jasmine. "But the very moment they do they become an occupying force. They have money, not men. No Royal of Heart is going to side with my family over one of their own."

Jasmine paused before reacting once again. Truly the wisest and most dangerous thing about her. "Aren't you both?"

"I'd be neither if you accept."

"Henri..." I uttered before even realizing it. The urge to make him not throw away what he had was strong, but my own pause to reflect made me smile. "You'd just be Henri."

He smiled at me, before turning back to Jasmine. "The deal must include both of us. Equally."

"Your Majesty," Hadi objected, and moved between me and the Princess as if to literally use his body to shield her. From this distance I smelled the twang of alcohol. "You can't let someone this dangerous into your court."

"You know just as well as I what is truly dangerous in Wonderland," Henri said poignantly. "Madison is as domesticated as anyone else. He's already served the Wolf King. And me. Your concern is misplaced."

Jasmine's bodyguard was a *currently* functioning alcoholic. Being able to drink the night away, and still be able to wake up early and command was its own type of magic. One that would not last forever and did not entitle him to give me shit. I bet if anything he's peed more inappropriate places than I ever had.

The Princess placed a hand on Hadi's shoulder as she stepped past him, coming into my view again. "Asylum seekers are meant to marry. Tasked with taking care of kids, or the future of the kingdom in some other way. Is this something you can do?"

"I'm certain we can work something out," said the soon-to-be-former Prince. "After all, you are the law here."

Jasmine returned Henri's pleased expression. "Come with me. Let's discuss it."

Henri kissed me on the cheek before he and Jasmine head off somewhere else. Most of the guards end up following, and Hadi dismissed a few more to check on remaining people in the bazaar. Until only he and a couple remain to watch me.

Hadi ends up staring at me as I stand there. Unable to resist, I stick out my tongue. The scoff that it gains makes him at least pretend to keep watch over the whole area, as if my immaturity proves I'm not a threat.

Boredom wins out as I end up in sitting down on the ground. "Hey, you!" I poke at air past Hadi, towards the other guard, Autar.

His mouth hung open for a second, unsure how to address me, maybe mentally searching for a title.

I decide to end his struggle before he figured one out. "How do things work around here?"

"Uh?" He glanced to Hadi, as if he was the answer. "Chain of command."

"Kinky."

Autar paled in an instant. For a second, he appears scandalized. Then his eyes nervously dart to his commander once more when Hadi isn't looking. There's something there, but I can't quite yet read what's between them as everyone falls into attention as Henri and Jasmine return.

She stops to give Hadi the papers, as Henri continued without pause to me.

"Hello, love," I said, getting back up to my feet. "Feared boredom might kill me as I waited."

"Well then, it's a good thing I know you'll come back to me if you had." *That I would.*

"Sorry, we took we bit," Henri continued. "We didn't go far, just to a café to sit and discuss."

"Never fear, you'll always be the Prince of *my* Heart."

"King."

"What?" My stomach lurched as I looked towards Jasmine. Did he marry himself off?

"Madison," Henri laughed, and placed a hand on my face to guide my eyes to back to him. "Will you make an honest man out of me?"

"You? Me? I—" Words were messy things that could not capture the complexity of what was being offered to me. Or at least not what I felt about it.

I picked Henri up at the waist, surprising him as he quickly held on with his arms around my neck. Even gave him a little boost so his legs could wrap around my hips.

He laughed more. "Is that a yes to marrying me?"

"It would be madness to say yes." I kissed him roughly was rewarded with a soft moan against my lips as he pressed himself into me further.

He looked dizzy as his mouth lifted from mine but held on just as tight. "Do you believe in marriage?"

"I believe in you."

His expression grows softer, full of happiness despite just trading everything he had away because of me.

Or maybe... Because he traded everything, he didn't really want in exchange for us. An unexpected future he actually wanted for himself.

"I'm going to show you so much love."

If you've enjoyed THE 9TH PAWN leave a review so other readers can know about Henri and Mads' romance!

READ MORE BIG BAD MAGIC
THE 10TH MASTER

A disgraced soldier.
A jinn who would still follow him anywhere.
And wishes neither of them can take back.

Turning a soldier under his command into a powerful jinn was never part of Hadi's military strategy. When that man is also your ex-boyfriend, suddenly planning the war effort is a welcome relief.

After refusing to return Autar's magical lamp to the cave of wonders, Hadi is exiled from the kingdom and must figure out a new life for himself. One that's dangerously tempting now that spoken desires become spellbound commands Autar must follow.

The plan was to sever the ties of their magical binding, but Hadi can't bring himself to wish for Autar to leave. And for a man who has already spent years under Hadi's leadership, Autar longs for his own wishes with this second chance at life and love. Can these two reconcile their broken relationship and build a whole new world together?

Keep the magic going with <u>THE 10TH MASTER</u> today!

ABOUT THE AUTHOR

Rose Sinclair writes stories filled with big magic, underworld romance, and queer characters who refuse to play by the rules. A community leader and activist at heart, they've spent over a decade shaking things up for LGBTQIA+ representation and building decentralized support networks. When they aren't busy masterminding their next fictional universe or hunting down rare trading cards, they can be found hanging out online. Connect with Rose on Instagram @RoseOverChaos.